"Want me to ask him about his fishing license?"

His gut twisted. Maybe paranoia from traveling with evidence, but something didn't sit right. "No, I don't—"

The fisherman turned, pulling a rifle from his side. "Nora, get down!" The bullets hit the water mere feet from the bow of the kayak. There was nowhere to hide. They were on the river without any cover, too easy a target. He struggled to duck and pull his weapon while sitting at an awkward angle in the cramped seat. A bullet hit the bow. Too close. He succeeded at releasing his gun and was lifting his arm to take aim when Nora twisted, taking her paddle with her. She placed her paddle to the right side of the boat as the gunman fired again, this time grazing the bow.

"Tandem roll," she yelled, then sucked in a breath and dove her head and body toward the water...

Heather Woodhaven earned her pilot's license, rode a hot-air balloon over the safari lands of Kenya, parasailed over Caribbean seas, lived through an accidental detour onto a black-diamond ski trail in Aspen, and snorkeled among stingrays before becoming a mother of three and wife of one. She channels her love for adventure into writing characters who find themselves in extraordinary circumstances.

Books by Heather Woodhaven

Love Inspired Suspense

Calculated Risk
Surviving the Storm
Code of Silence
Countdown
Texas Takedown
Tracking Secrets
Credible Threat
Protected Secrets
Wilderness Sabotage
Deadly River Pursuit

Twins Separated at Birth

Undercover Twin
Covert Christmas Twin

True Blue K-9 Unit: Brooklyn

Chasing Secrets

Visit the Author Profile page at Harlequin.com.

DEADLY RIVER PURSUIT

HEATHER WOODHAVEN

LOVE INSPIRED SUSPENSE
INSPIRATIONAL ROMANCE

LOVE INSPIRED® SUSPENSE
INSPIRATIONAL ROMANCE

ISBN-13: 978-1-335-40509-8

Recycling programs
for this product may
not exist in your area.

Deadly River Pursuit

Copyright © 2021 by Heather Humrichouse

This edition published by arrangement with Harlequin Books S.A.

For questions and comments about the quality of this book, please contact us
at CustomerService@Harlequin.com.

Love Inspired
22 Adelaide St. West, 40th Floor
Toronto, Ontario M5H 4E3, Canada
www.Harlequin.com

Printed in U.S.A.

Bear ye one another's burdens,
and so fulfil the law of Christ.
—*Galatians* 6:2

To my family. Thank you for researching and adventuring
with me...and understanding my need for hotels
and indoor plumbing at the end of the day.

ONE

The Killer was just around the bend.

Categorized as Class III rapids, The Killer attracted whitewater enthusiasts to the Sauvage River. To the best of Nora Radley's knowledge, no one had ever actually been killed by the rapids, though the name served as a warning to those who didn't have the knowledge or experience to stay away.

Her torso twisted ever so slightly from the waist as she cut the paddle through the calm portion of the crystal-clear spring waters. The blue kayak responded immediately to her movement and changed course. The heavy snowmelt added several feet of water, which could produce newfound dangers before the official rafting season started.

This year's examination of the river held extra importance. As acting manager of The Sauvage Run Rafting Company, Nora's marketing efforts had been unsuccessful until *Wonder Travel Magazine* announced they were sending a journalist to Idaho to experience the early season's opening weekend run. The publicity might be her only shot at getting her aunt's business back to profitable.

She rested the paddle on top of the kayak and savored the floating sensation. The moment she was back on the river, it was like returning home, or at least what she imagined the feeling of home to be like. Her heart flooded with excitement as she rounded the bend. The roar reached her ears before she spotted the giant waves, still a good hundred yards or so in the distance.

To her left, Sandy Cape's beach didn't jut into the river as far as last year. Concerning but still workable. The beach served as the first stop for guests to eat lunch and marvel at the wild rapids before they ventured forth. She fought against a disappointed groan, anxious to keep going, but she had a job to do.

She maneuvered her paddle and aimed for land. A raft, on the opposite end of the beach, poked out from between two boulders. *The Sauvage Run* was printed in dark blue on the side. She clenched her jaw. None of the employees was supposed to take out a raft without her knowledge.

Nora gave the paddle an extra shove on the right and ramped up onto the sand.

"It's pretty simple. All of the cash at the—"

The waves sloshed against the back end of her kayak so she couldn't hear the rest. The voice had to belong to Dexter Miller, the sharp-edged tone a dead giveaway. She already regretted hiring him. If it turned out he was soliciting money under the table for private rafting trips when he should be in training, Nora's patience would reach its end, even if her aunt had pushed for the hire.

She stepped out of the kayak and dragged it the rest of the way onto the sand. Just past the firepit and picnic tables, she spotted Dexter among the trees, still talking with his trademark arrogance, but she couldn't see the other person.

"The ball's in your court, but if I go missing then you don't get your stuff," Dexter said, his chin jutting upward.

What kind of racket was Dexter trying to pull? The defiance and lack of respect seemed woven in the fiber of his bones. Most of the guides were young and Nora expected a certain amount of immaturity, but Dexter was in his forties. "I have a good guess how much it's worth," Dexter continued. "I guarantee you won't be able to find—"

"You got to say your piece," a man remarked, his voice low and monotone. "Now, it's my turn. See that over there?"

Nora squinted, trying to get a glimpse of the other man. She had a feeling she knew that voice but couldn't place it. She continued forward, the downward pull of the sand impeding her progress. Another step allowed her to see the back of the other man through the branches. Black jacket, brown hair, average height, but nothing indicated his identity yet. Interrupting their conversation wasn't her first choice, but she also wanted to make her presence known lest they assume she was intentionally eavesdropping.

The man lifted a gun while Dexter looked at something to the southeast. A shot rang out.

Her chest seized in a gasp. The greeting she'd been

about to holler caught in the back of her throat. Dexter crumpled to the ground. The man spun, pulling up a gray camouflage mask as he turned. The sun reflected off something in his hand, probably the gun, and the blue lenses of the dark sunglasses covered the rest of his face. He raised his arm.

Nora ducked instinctively. A bullet hit a rock a foot from where she was standing. She sprinted across the shore, pumping her arms as hard as possible, despite the restrictive nature of the wet suit. Going back to her kayak, which was sitting out in the open on the sandy beach, wasn't an option. Another shot rang out, producing an explosion of sand against her shins.

She slid as if going for home base until she was behind the largest boulder on the farthest side of the beach. Her insides vibrated and she struggled to focus on her options. One more step and she'd sink into the water, which had to be a good eight-feet deep. The current would drag her right into the rapids. She situated herself in a crouch. The wind gusted and a wave slapped her back and neck, the sudden chill hard to ignore.

If she tried to climb the rocks to get to the wooded area, her head would be exposed, but she couldn't stay put. Should the gunman walk this way, she'd be an easy target. The raft Dexter had precariously parked on top of loose rock between two boulders sat a few feet away. His reckless, lazy choice might be her only chance at survival.

The only way off Sandy Cape was on the raft, through The Killer. She'd never be able to say the name of the rapids with a laugh again. Trying to stay crouched while crawling up the loose rock proved useless. Gravity pulled her back toward the water. Her outstretched fingers snagged the perimeter rope threaded through the D-rings on the outside of the raft. The boat skated down after her, taking a handful of rocks with it.

She managed to sidestep just enough to dive into the raft and hunker down on the floor. The current grabbed the boat instantly. It wasn't the safest place to be as she approached the rapids, but it was safer than being hit by a bullet.

Nora propped up on her knees and clutched the handles of the two oars while trying to stay low. The rapids would be even harder to manage with only her weight in the raft, which was big enough for four people. She stole a glance at the beach. Was the gunman coming after her in the kayak she'd left behind? Or would he try to climb the rocks and shoot at her again?

A three-foot wave collapsed over the bow of the raft, flipping it over. Her fingers grazed the outside of the boat as it tipped over, catching the perimeter rope as water rushed over her head. She fought against the aerated water that wanted to toss her about under the surface. The moment her head broke free, she pulled in a breath and held tight to the taut rope. Almost on autopilot, she managed to flip the raft and hoist herself up and into it. That second-long glance at the beach had cost her.

She laid flat, sputtering, until she caught her breath. But there was no time to waste as the worst of the rapids was still to come. She pushed upright on one knee, twisted into a seated position at the back and grabbed the oars. Gunman or not, she would die if she didn't focus on the turbulent waters.

The river had changed with the snowmelt and she needed to find a current to take to get out of the rapids as soon as possible. Interlocking ridges and valleys bordered the Sauvage River. If she waited even a half mile more downriver to get out, she would enter a canyon and, without other people to help her maneuver the large raft, there were would be no easy exit off the water for miles.

She needed to call for help but couldn't afford to take a hand off an oar. The safest path to land would take her to the same side of the river as the gunman. Almost like a giant V in the river, another path presented itself, barely skirting a boulder poking out of the water. With four quick strokes, Nora maneuvered into the current and braced herself to stay on top of the roller coaster of waves. A minute later, instead of laughing—like all rafters after an exhilarating ride—she stumbled out of the raft onto a north-side bank.

Pulling in giant breaths and spinning to look over her shoulder every few steps, she dragged the raft up behind her. Her chest heaved and her eyes burned, but she refused to stop and cry. She couldn't. What if Dexter was still alive? She hadn't actually seen him get shot, but she'd heard it, seen him fall. If there was a chance he could be saved, every second counted.

Her shaky hands unzipped the pocket on the side of her suit. The satellite phone didn't always grab a signal near the high canyon walls and thick tree canopy. *Please*. She dialed and, mercifully, the county dispatcher answered.

Nora didn't wait for questions. "A man shot one of my guides at Sandy Cape." She stepped into the cover of the trees, watching the river for signs she'd been followed. "I don't know if he's still alive or not." Her body started trembling, then her arms and legs began shaking more violently. Likely from the frigid water and the adrenaline. A natural reaction, she told herself. She tried inhaling and exhaling deeply to calm her mind so her body would relax, but it wasn't working. Her teeth chattered. "The shooter might follow me. I left my kayak there. I had to."

"Ma'am, where are you now?"

"Um—" Nora turned around "—the emergency takeout. Closest to Clair Creek."

"Okay, can you make your way to the road? I have an officer en route to you."

"Yes, but you also need to send someone to Sandy Cape—"

"Ma'am, Sandy Cape is only accessible by boat. I've got a call out to the forest service and the search and rescue team."

Sandy Cape was on US Forest Service land, all south of the river. Nora took measured steps through the overgrown foliage, around slippery rocks and past crooked pine trees, until she spotted the thin dirt trail only used when a rafter had to finish early. She was currently north of the river, on Bureau of Land Management property. She trudged forward, the phone still against her ear. The search and rescue team was based in the small town of Sauvage, six miles north of her rafting company. They were well trained, but all volunteers with day jobs. "If you wait for search and rescue, that won't be fast enough to save Dex—"

The line went dead. No signal.

The sound of a motor approached. No sirens.

She tensed, ready to run, and rounded the hill dotted with sage and patches of snow on the north side.

A tan pickup drove at full speed, dust and rocks spewing from the tires.

She dropped her head. *No. Please not him. Anyone but him.*

Henry McKnight pressed his lips together as he took the full impact of the dirt road's bumps at high-speed. He'd been nearby investigating an illegal trash dump when he'd heard the call for assistance. A rafting guide in danger after witnessing a shooting.

He gripped the wheel tighter, unwilling to reduce his speed as he raced to the location Dispatch had described. Another rafting guide wasn't going to be murdered on his watch. He felt the burden of the cold case all over again.

A rafting guide and friend, Tommy Sorenson, had been murdered ten years ago. In fact, Tommy's death had been the very reason Henry had trained to become a law enforcement ranger for the Bureau of Land Management.

A flash of light reflected off the sheen of the raft a young lady carried over her head. His foot slipped off the gas pedal. His ex-fiancée, Nora? He blinked and pressed the gas pedal forward, though not at as high a speed. Her life jacket dangled from the crook in her arm. She walked at a slow pace in purple water shoes.

Had Dispatch been wrong? She didn't act like a woman in danger. Perhaps he was in the wrong place.

As he grew closer, the strain in Nora's posture became visible. She didn't even offer a fake smile, which he'd come to expect on the rare occasion they'd bumped into each other.

He pulled to a stop, careful not to get close enough his truck would spray her with dust. He hopped out, his hand on his weapon. The dispatcher had said the shooter might still be after the guide. "Are you okay?" He knew his question sounded abrupt, and he regretted the tone of his voice the instant her eyes widened. But the thought of someone shooting at her felt like lava in the pit of his stomach.

"Not really," she said, blinking rapidly. She pulled back her shoulders and nodded resolutely, as if flipping a switch to turn off her emotions. "Don't worry about me. A man shot one of my guides, Dexter Miller, and you know how long search and rescue can take to deploy—"

"Get in." Henry took the raft from her and secured it in the back of his pickup, moving as fast as his hands would allow. His fingers shook ever so slightly when he was this agitated, which wasn't helpful in securing the tie-downs. He took a deep breath, but his eyes kept flashing to the trees. He felt the shortage of law enforcement daily. The entire region had less than a dozen officers, some part-time at that, working for the sheriff's office. Given that the county was almost twice the size of the state of Rhode Island, both the Bureau of Land Management and the United States Forest Service had active law contracts with the department. They needed all the help they could get.

He joined Nora in the front and put the truck in Drive. "The dispatcher said Sandy Cape was where the shooting happened?" He spun the vehicle around, narrowly avoiding a fallen log. He placed a comforting hand on Nora's arm out of habit. She glanced down at his hand, her frown deepening. He immediately pulled back. "You're safe now," he said stiffly, trying to cover over his faux pas.

He steered back onto the dirt road to the closest highway. Sandy Cape was technically on USFS land. Hopefully, Dispatch had already sent word to the Enforcement Investigations officer, Perry Fletcher. Then again, Perry might be in the middle of nowhere without so much as a satellite signal.

"What'd the shooter look like?" Henry asked Nora.

"I don't know. His face was covered with a gray camouflage mask." Nora fingered her pink tube scarf, now bunched at the base of her neck. The scarves, made of lightweight material, were favored by outdoor enthusiasts as they could be worn a myriad of ways. "He wore sunglasses, too. I didn't get a good look at his face. Black jacket. Medium build, I think."

He grabbed the radio with a side glance. "Anything else you can tell me?"

"He—" She placed a hand on her forehead and closed

her eyes. "I'm sorry. It happened so fast. I can't stop thinking about Dexter."

He clicked the radio on and informed the dispatcher that he was taking Nora to The Sauvage Run Rafting Company.

"No, please," Nora said, a bite to her voice. "If you take me back, it'll be a good hour before you get to Sandy Cape."

"You need to get back first."

She crossed her arms. "Please don't make assumptions where I'm concerned."

He fought against a cringe. He knew she was referring to the events leading to their breakup.

"Do you at least have river patrol ready to take you there?" Nora asked.

"No." He knew but didn't tell her that they weren't hiring an intern until later in the year, if they even received a qualified application.

Nora folded her arms over her chest. "You need a river guide. I interned once for your boss. He left the door open for me to take a river patrol position anytime."

"That was five years ago, Nora, and—"

"If you tell the deputies to meet us at the next creek, I can get you to Sandy Cape fast. The raft is big enough for four of us." Her eyes softened. "If there's any chance to save my guide…"

"Deputies, meet me at Petillant Creek," he said into the radio with a sigh.

"Thank you," she said softly.

"I still don't want you involved. If you loan us your

raft, I can take it and one of the deputies can take you back to the lodge."

"Who would guide?"

He hesitated. Technically, he probably could, but it had been ten years since he'd run the river.

"It's high water at its fiercest right now." Nora reached over and flipped off the air vents, her lips tinged with blue. The March air was warmer than usual, but probably didn't feel that way after a spill in the rapids. "I've been training all winter," Nora continued. "All my safety certs are up to date. Besides, my kayak is still there. Hopefully. Henry, I know it's not ideal, but if I'm Dexter's best chance at getting help…"

"Fine. Only because it's an emergency. You can guide us there for the sake of time, but you'll have to stay with the boat while we investigate." He'd let his swift-water rescue certifications fall on the back burner, and Nora knew his secret. Even though they'd met and fallen in love when they were both river guides in their college years, Henry had finished the summer by rafting right into a boulder. With his leg hanging on the outside of the raft, he'd snapped his tibia. The experience had gifted him with a newfound fear of whitewater rafting.

He'd been on the river since then but never as a guide. Most of the river management went to the forest service, except for the additional help BLM River Patrol offered in the summers, usually from an intern because they hadn't found someone on staff willing to work long hours for three months of the year. Nora had once said she would love to do the job every summer when she transitioned to teaching. But as far as Henry knew, she'd never stopped working for her aunt.

"You can help today, but I'm not going to take your river patrol offer seriously. You *are* still working for your aunt?"

Nora sighed. "Yes. She's in Alaska right now, taking care of her sick cousin and getting some time to herself."

Henry had heard the rumors but didn't comment. Most of the town knew about Nora's uncle—well, ex-uncle now—and his philandering ways that had led to the divorce. Didn't stop Frank Milner from getting re-elected as a county commissioner, though.

Henry found the creek entrance and made his way there. They kept busy pulling the boat out of the truck and outfitting it with his first-aid kit. Two deputies pulled up behind them in an SUV.

He glanced at Nora. "Are you sure you're up for this?"

She bit her lip and nodded. "I just hope we make it in time."

Her comment sounded more like a question and sent a chill up his spine. Their eyes met, and he saw the hope fading there. Henry's hand went instinctively to his gun as he thought about the shooter. There was a chance the gunman was still out there, and if Nora was a witness, Henry would do whatever it took to keep her out of danger.

TWO

Nora grabbed the oars, impatient for the deputies to get into the raft. The adrenaline was fading, replaced with a war of conflicting emotions about being around Henry again. It'd been several years since they'd stood in the parking lot of the lodge, after yet another disagreement, and Henry had gently suggested they take a break. With those words, the engagement had ended and they'd never talked about it since. Maybe if her heart would finally get over him, it would be easier to be herself whenever he was near.

Two deputies kicked up dust as they made their way over. With low pay and too much work, law enforcement in the area didn't last long before transferring elsewhere. Most of the deputies the sheriff did keep on staff were relatively young. Deputy Zach O'Brien was no exception. A relatively new hire, he'd only lived in the area a couple years. He wore a freshly trimmed goatee and had steely gray eyes. "We left Carl's car at the Clair Creek take-out for when we're done."

"Good idea," Henry said.

"Hi, Carl," Nora said with a wave. Carl Alexander,

the other deputy, was only a few years younger than she and had grown up in Sauvage. He'd worked in summer rafting as well, as most teens in the area were encouraged to try their hand at guiding. He'd worked for her uncle's company, though, the only other rafting company on the Sauvage River.

Carl had always been quiet, a good listener, and seemed like the type to be slow to anger. Qualities that made him a good cop contrasted with Zach's loud and obnoxious persona that set her teeth on edge. Carl nodded a greeting and stepped in the raft.

Henry glanced at his sport watch, likely worried about the time. The later they hit the water, the later they would get back to the take-out spot. Getting stuck on the rapids in the dark was to be avoided at all costs.

"I'm going to need everyone's help if we're to hit the fastest currents." She could cut the time it'd take to get to Sandy Cape by at least half if they worked hard. She pointed to the seat right in front of her. "Henry can sit there. Deputy Alexander and Deputy O'Brien, you take either side of the bow."

Henry flashed her an irritated glance but did as she said. The spot she'd assigned him was the least likely to dump into the water. She thought he'd appreciate the gesture, but it wasn't a big surprise that they didn't see eye to eye anymore.

Their strong connection had stopped the moment he'd moved back to the area as a law enforcement ranger. That's where all their problems had started. He'd changed, just like everyone who'd warned her against long-distance relationships had said he would. She just hadn't seen it until he'd hauled her and her sister, Maya, into the sheriff's office like common criminals when they'd done nothing wrong.

The wind gusted, a reminder that it was time to be mindful of the work ahead. Nora would usually pull up her tube scarf to use as a face cover, but it was too reminiscent of the style the shooter had worn so she left it on her neck. Only one small set of rapids stood in their way before Sandy Cape. Radios crackled between the three men, and they took turns answering, presumably communicating to Dispatch.

She spotted her kayak, untouched, her helmet and paddle still resting on top. Like everything about the business, Nora was responsible for employee safety and the new rafts and kayaks her aunt had purchased from the meager bookings of last year. Hope surged that Dexter would be safe, too.

They gave a final push with the oars and the raft slid onto the bank.

A man stepped out of the trees with a wave. "Over here!"

Even without the tell-tale green uniform, Nora would've recognized the man's husky voice. Perry Fletcher worked for the forest service Law Enforcement Investigations unit. While a good fifteen years older, he'd served as a mentor to Henry, helping solidify his decision to abandon law school and pursue a career as a law enforcement ranger. Back when Nora still believed in happily-ever-after.

Henry and the deputies joined Perry at the tree line. She stayed at the side of the raft, searching the trees for any sign of a hidden shooter. The way the men gathered and looked over their shoulders, sympathy in their eyes, Nora didn't need to ask.

Dexter was dead.

"Suicide?" Henry's voice carried. He placed two fists on his waist.

Nora rushed forward. "What? No, I saw—"

Perry stepped forward, blocking her progress to the tree line. "I don't think you should get closer, Nora. It's not a pretty sight. He didn't make it."

Her breath grew shallow. "But why did Henry say suicide? There was a man. He shot Dexter. I saw it."

Perry studied her face, empathy lining his features. "Where were you standing when you saw the man, Nora?"

"Right about here." Nora looked over Perry's shoulder to where Henry and the deputies stood. A black jacket hung on a set of tree branches. The wind gusted, making the sleeves move slightly. "That jacket wasn't there before. I mean the killer might've left it—"

"Don't you usually wear glasses?" Perry tilted his head and studied her. He aimed a thumb over his shoulders at the trees and rocks behind him. "I approached with my gun at the ready because I thought I saw a man at first, too, so I understand. But upon investigation, all the indications…"

"I'm wearing contacts." Her throat tightened and her chest seized. She *knew* what she'd seen, and it hadn't been a jacket blowing in the wind. "What indications? I saw—"

"A shot to the side of the head at such a close contact is usually indicative—"

"The man told Dexter to look at something and shot him."

"A man in a black jacket?" The look of pity made her want to scream. Perry ignored her glare and ticked off his fingers. "The distance of the shot from the body caused a burn mark around the wound. It was at contact range. The angle of the shot was slightly upward, as if self-inflicted. It was only one shot, and the gun is in the victim's hand. Those all make this less likely to be homicide."

"They were standing close to each other. So, when Dexter looked away the man must have put the gun against the side of his head to make it look like a suicide."

"Perry," Henry called out, "can I talk to you for a moment?"

The ranger shrugged and turned as if to go to Henry but spun back around to Nora. "You're a week early in scouting the river, aren't you? The other company hasn't even started."

Nora really didn't feel like chatting with Perry at the moment when he didn't seem to believe her, but the rafting business relied on a good relationship with the forest service. "We have a special visitor coming. It's important for our first early season run to be perfect." She didn't see the need to explain her aunt's financial predicament to Perry, though.

"A mudslide brought down a boulder the size of a semi right before the take-out near Garnet Rapids. It's right in the path of the most used current, so extra dangerous. Search for a new path or you're guaranteed to high side and get stranded on that rock. Let me know what you find out so I can alert the other rafting company. We might have to cut down some foliage for an earlier take-out point if it's too dangerous."

She struggled to make note of Perry's advice over the rage coursing through her veins. The shooter she'd seen hadn't been a jacket in a tree. Though, with the shadows, the bark could be misconstrued as the gray camouflage… She blinked. No, her eyes hadn't tricked her. And she had *heard* them arguing. She couldn't have imagined that.

Could she have?

Henry waited impatiently for Perry to finish talking with Nora before they stepped out of earshot. While both land management organizations had a partnership regarding the river and the rafters, Sandy Cape was clearly Perry's jurisdiction. He could wave Henry and the deputies away in favor of the FBI or no help at all, so Henry knew he needed to tread carefully. "If you don't mind me asking, how'd you get here so fast?" he asked. "I thought there were no motor vehicles allowed."

Perry puffed up his chest. "I was nearby at the Martin ranch, taking a witness statement about trespassers. Likely more mobile meth labs in the making." He shook his head, before he exhaled and smirked. "Official business enables me to use an ATV when it's absolutely necessary. Let's just say there are benefits to being on the right side of public land management."

Henry fought against rolling his eyes at the well-played dig. There was a good-natured rivalry between their organizations. "Did you keep a lookout for any other tracks on your way here?"

Perry widened his stance. "Dispatch thought there might've been a chance the victim was still alive after being shot, so I deemed it necessary to drive my ATV as fast as I could. I was trying to save what I thought was a dying man."

"So that's a no." Henry regretted saying the thought aloud instantly.

"I think my dedication speaks for itself." Perry's eyes hardened. "Look, why is Nora even here? You could've gotten her statement without bringing her back to the scene."

"She helped us get here faster and, like you, we thought there was a chance to save the victim. I believe she saw something, Perry."

He blew out a breath and shook his head. "I probably shouldn't have discussed theories with her, but I honestly thought there was a man there, too, when I approached. I don't blame her in the slightest for thinking it was murder."

"She said she heard two men talking."

Perry shrugged. "We both know eyewitnesses make mistakes. Our brains trick us into making sense of things, especially in the heat of the moment. The wind through the trees, the birds, the squirrels, they can sound like voices when I'm on patrol. And since Tommy Sorenson was murdered at a rafting stop it's only natural for her mind to fill in—"

Perry's radio went off, and he turned down the volume. "The point is, you don't need to tell me how to do my job, Henry. I also don't need Nora telling everyone she witnessed a murder. That'd turn the area into a media circus that will only hurt our already depressed economy. We don't need our bosses to breathe down our necks for answers we don't have."

"Is that what happened when Tommy was killed?" Henry knew he was on thin ice, but Tommy's murder had happened on Forest Service soil, as well.

Perry pressed his lips together for a moment. "Same lack of resources back then, too, but you didn't stick around to see how news of a rafting guide's murder devastated the economy for several years after the fact. I've got over a hundred open cases right now. These mobile meth labs keep popping up faster than I can shut down—"

Henry held up a hand to shorten a rant he understood all too well. "We've all got a big load. I don't want it to be murder, either, but we can't write off an eyewitness to suit our need to close the case fast."

Perry pursed his lips, as if about to argue, but he relaxed instead. "We're on the same page. I'll assign the sheriff's deputies to interview the other rafting guides and town businesses. Let's get a handle on who the victim was to see if we can find a motive for either scenario while we wait for the lab to analyze the evidence."

"Search and rescue just came around the bend," Nora called out.

"Get her home," Perry said to Henry, this time softer. "Take her official statement, and maybe we'll find something concrete to go on. I need to process the scene before it gets any later in the day." They both glanced at the horizon. Processing a scene took hours, and spring sunsets in the mountains happened early. Time was running out.

"Understood." There would be more deputies on the boat to help take over the processing of the scene. Carl was already wrapping crime scene tape around trees. "I'll take her home and make sure the other rafting company knows Sandy Cape is off-limits for now."

Perry tilted his head in the direction of the river. "We all like Nora." His voice and face relaxed into the thoughtful ranger Henry respected. "If her eyes weren't playing tricks on her, then I suppose it's possible someone planted the jacket to cast doubt. I still say it's unlikely, but I'm sure you'll keep an eye on her."

He read between the lines. When Nora and Henry had broken the engagement, Perry had predicted it would only be temporary, lasting a month tops. The memory served as a reminder that his mentor and friend could be very wrong at times. It'd been almost three years since they'd split up.

The other deputies and volunteer firemen of the search and rescue team hit the sand. Nora rushed forward to help secure the raft. Henry helped the team pull out the collapsible stretcher and gear Perry would need to transport the body.

Zach approached and nodded at the abandoned kayak near the rocks. "Carl is almost done collecting evidence. He offered to take your kayak back."

Nora nodded. "He regularly kayaks on the river, doesn't he?"

"As far as I know." Zach hopped in the raft. "I'm supposed to accompany you back. Glad we're not looking at murder. Not good for business. Not good at all."

Henry shot a dark look at him, but the deputy didn't take the hint and continued to offer his commentary as the three of them set off.

Nora pursed her lips and guided them through The Killer with hardly any instructions.

Henry's leg produced a phantom pain with every wave, remembering the sensation of his tibia snapping when he'd hit the boulder at full speed. He gritted his teeth.

His accident had happened shortly after Tommy had been killed, and Henry had wrestled with guilt for not taking his friend seriously when he'd started acting like something bad was going to happen to him.

"Move left!" Nora hollered.

Henry leaned as Nora deftly avoided a swirling, churning hydraulic and the raft leveled. He exhaled, but his muscles wouldn't relax. Moments later, she steered the boat onto the same emergency take-out at Clair Creek where he'd found her hours before.

Zach had the keys to the SUV that'd been left there. They attached the raft to the roof and got back on the road. Deputy O'Brien never had a shortage of words and since his wife had recently taken over running the bistro in town, he told stories of her experiments with new menus and fonts. Nora politely nodded but said nothing.

Zach dropped them off at Henry's truck, still at Petillant Creek, and turned around to go back to pick up the search and rescue crew.

Nora finally spoke. "I admire your courage."

"What?" Henry pulled his chin back, surprised at the change. "For what?"

She averted her eyes. "I know you hate the rapids. You practically turned green when we first got in the boat. Does it still hurt?" She gestured to his leg.

"Only occasionally. I feel like an old man when I can predict a storm before the weatherman."

Her smile warmed his insides in a way nothing else had for years. "You don't think I could've imagined it, do you?"

He squeezed his hands tighter around the steering wheel and focused on the road. "Do you?"

She crossed her arms over her chest. "A jacket in the wind doesn't make a person imagine being shot at."

He braked hard and twisted to face her. "Nora, you never said anything about getting shot at!"

"I did, too!" She opened her mouth wide and her eyes darted side to side as if she was rewinding her thoughts. "I told the dispatcher that I was afraid the shooter was still coming after me."

Henry rubbed his forehead, trying not to let his frustration boil over. Nora had stopped talking to him, stopped sharing her thoughts, months before their breakup, so maybe she hadn't been more forthcoming because he was the one on the case. To be fair, she was also the type of person to not detail all of her symptoms to a doctor because "he's the professional." She likely thought her statement was being ignored at the crime scene, especially after Perry's rant. And, sadly, this kind of slip was a consequence of having three separate law enforcement agencies working a scene. Details slid through the cracks. "Is it possible you didn't tell Dispatch that the man actually shot *at* you?"

She bit her lip and stared ahead for a second. "I'm sorry. It all happened so fast."

The light was fading. "I'll call Perry, and we'll return to the scene in the morning." He focused on the road and merged onto the paved highway where he could increase his speed, though he had to slow down for all the sharp curves around the foothills. "Someone will be sent from the sheriff's office to look through Dexter's things and ask more questions. It might be later tonight or first thing in the morning, but it will be soon."

She nodded. "I figured. I have his family contact information somewhere."

"One of the deputies will likely contact them," he said.

"I feel like I should reach out, too." Her voice wavered. "I can't help but think about Tommy Sorenson's death." Her shoulders sagged, and she turned to look out the window.

He was thinking the same thing, but they weren't at the place to talk like the best friends they used to be. "I need to take your official statement once we get to the lodge, if you're up for it."

"I've already told you everything I know."

"We missed that the shooter tried to kill you, so clearly we have more to discuss." Henry hated to admit it, but for her safety, it might be better for another officer to interview her anyway. She might be more free with her testimony. He pulled into the parking lot.

Nora blew out a slow breath. "Okay. Dexter told the shooter that if anything happened to him, the guy wouldn't get his stuff. Then the shooter said it was his turn to talk, and shot him." She continued to stare out the window. "I think I'd really like to call it a night. Maybe I'll remember more details tomorrow." Her voice trembled.

It was as if he'd been punched in the gut. He was desperate to help, to comfort, to fix it. He started to reach for her hand and stopped himself. He'd been down this path before and couldn't fall for her again. "Thanks again for getting us to the scene fast. A deputy will be by tonight or first thing in the morning. Make sure you lock up."

She glanced at him and her eyes looked red, as if holding back tears. She waved goodbye and disappeared into the rafting office without a word.

Henry sat in the parking lot for a moment to organize his swirling thoughts.

Nora had been a witness to a murder. There was no question in his mind. Someone had shot at her, which meant the shooter was still at large. His mouth went dry. Nora would be pretty easy to find. No matter their history, he couldn't stand by and let her be in danger. He shifted the truck into Drive and sped off. There was a lot to do if he had any hope of keeping her safe.

THREE

Nora flipped on the office light and the small porta-ble heater. In the summer, they lifted the wall, much like a garage door, for guests to come in and out as they pleased, but in the spring, the office resembled a private cabin. She stared at the filing cabinet, the bane of her existence. Her aunt wasn't ready to go paperless and had been the one to hand over Dexter's application. The police would likely need it for his next-of-kin in-formation. She opened the desk drawer where she kept the cabinet key.

The front door swung open. Bobby Olson stepped in-side, his tanned skin complementing the neon-orange shirt that read Eat, Sleep, Raft, Repeat. His hair looked per-manently windswept and sun-bleached, hanging just past his chin line. A little over fifty-five years old, Bobby was their oldest and most experienced guide, returning every season. During the winter months, he moved to Chile to raft the rivers there. He was never without a story and a joke, which made him a favorite among the clientele.

A line between his eyebrows appeared that she'd never seen on him before. "Are you okay?"

She averted eye contact. "You heard already."

"That you found Dexter? Yeah." He nodded. "It's already all over town. I won't speak ill of the dead. Even if I didn't like him, it's still tragic." He shook his head. "Suicide was hard to believe, though. It's a shock."

She bit the inside of her cheek to keep quiet. That's what everyone wanted from her. To stay quiet because murder could cause panic and hurt the fragile economy, but she'd never promised to hold her peace. If she couldn't tell Bobby, then who was left? She had no confidante or friend nearby anymore. Maybe if she talked, the horrible strain in her throat would go away.

"This stays between us, Bobby. I saw someone shoot Dexter. When I took the police back to the crime scene, it had been set up to look like a suicide. It was made to appear as if I'd just seen things. But the gunman shot at me, too, when I saw him. I couldn't have imagined that, right?"

"Of course not." Bobby's eyes practically popped before he pulled his chin back and regained his relaxed demeanor. "Of all the imaginative people I've ever met, you are not one of them."

"Thanks—" She replayed his words. "Maybe?"

He winked and smiled. "What I mean is you are as reliable as a person gets. You get done what needs done without much thought to what *you* want. You're not prone to starry-eyed dreams, and you don't imagine gunmen shooting at you." He crossed his arms at his chest. "So, I'm going to ask again. Are you okay?"

Her confidence grew as Bobby spoke. "Yes. I'm not looking forward to reliving it all when the police come by, but yes. I'm okay." She noticed his frown had returned. Bobby was in charge of training the new guides while her aunt was gone, and today should've been a day entirely in the classroom, going over basic first aid. The recruits trained for a week during their respective spring breaks then began working weekends until summer break. "Is there something you wanted to tell *me*?"

"I figured you should probably be aware that Frank is trying to steal your employees again."

She threw her head back and groaned. Of course he was. Why couldn't Bobby have been her uncle instead? No wonder Aunt Linda needed some time away after the divorce. She knew how Frank Milner worked, quick to take advantage of new circumstances. But finding quality employees—usually college students—became a tougher challenge each year. "Let me guess. He expressed concern that our employees would have a hard time staying here what with memories of Dexter."

"He offered them a place without reminders." Bobby nodded. "So far, no one has taken him up on it." He sighed. "But no one's heard it's murder yet, and that might change things. Police can't keep that under wraps for long. Have you called your aunt yet?"

"Not yet." In fact, she couldn't imagine doing so. "This might upset her. I think I've got it under control."

His shoulders drooped. "It's not your job to keep everyone happy, Nora. Linda is a strong woman. She started this business before you came along, you know. I think she can handle it." Bobby tilted his head. "Did I see Henry drop you off? Is he concerned the shooter might come after you?"

"He didn't say anything." Her spine straightened.

The shooter coming after her had never entered her mind until now. The unprocessed emotions around Henry and the murder would be her undoing if she didn't stop thinking about them.

Her computer dinged with an email from *Wonder Travel Magazine*. Condolences and possible reschedule? How did the magazine already know about Dexter's death? This was too much.

"You've had a rough day. We can talk later." Bobby put one hand on the door handle. "Do yourself a favor and take it easy tonight. I've got tonight under control." He slipped outside and gathered the guides to make dinner at the back edge of the property. The first wave of trainees would learn how to make the most scrumptious meals over a fire. Not even the promise of Bobby's BBQ chicken could entice her, though.

She'd save the email for tomorrow when she could hopefully handle it and made her way to her room, eager to be alone. The employee lodge was like a one-floor coed dormitory. Centered by the main entrance, the female section of rooms were on the left and the male section on the right.

She couldn't resist walking past Dexter's room once even though the door was locked as she expected. Her room was located closest to the front door. Larger than the other accommodations provided to the guides, her place resembled a miniature apartment with a living room the size of a walk-in closet, a private bathroom that compared to those sized for RVs, and a kitchenette. She'd been sharing the space since she was fifteen with her younger sister, until Maya left.

Aunt Linda had lived in the one-room apartment above the camping office until she'd met and married Frank and moved into a giant house in the foothills that overlooked the town and river. It had been an unusual arrangement for a teenager compared to the homes her friends had lived in, but Nora's life had been anything but normal.

Once dry and warm in her coziest set of flannel pajamas, she slept fitfully. She woke multiple times in the night, remembering the sound of the bullets and the way the sand stung her ankles as she'd run away. On the fifth time the nightmare reoccurred, she'd had enough of the tossing and turning. She sat up and glanced at her phone. Four in the morning.

A thud sounded from somewhere in the dormitory. Odd. She saw a sliver of light flash from under her door.

She slid into her slippers, grabbed her phone and key lanyard and made her way to the door. Occasionally guides got locked out of their room while using the restroom and she would be called upon to get the master key. Since she was already up, she'd rather be the one to take care of it rather than have someone waking Bobby. He always did a final safety check and locked up the place, so he would've been up late. She opened her door a crack.

The hallway was pitch black except for the patches of moonlight, broken up by the trees, streaming in through the glass on the front door like a night-light. She took a step into the hallway, squinting. Another thud followed by a scrape. She shuffled down the hallway, irritation growing. She may have already been awake, but if the guide didn't stop making noise, he might wake the others. Light from under one of the doors in the men's section caught her attention. Her mouth went dry. Wasn't that Dexter's room?

The light extinguished, and the door opened. Every muscle tensed as she faced the silhouette stepping out of the room. In the darkness all she could make out was a man's form, but she couldn't get her eyes to widen enough. It appeared he had no face.

She clicked the button on the side of her phone and the light from the screen illuminated her feet as she began to lift her arm. "Who are—?"

The figure sprang at her, slamming her backward. Her shoulders felt the brunt of the attack, as if two bowling balls had been launched at her. She stumbled back so quickly, her feet left the slippers behind. The forceful push proved too intense to keep her balance. She dropped, twisting her right arm back to catch herself.

Her elbow hit the carpeted hallway first before her back slammed against the floor followed by her head. Pain radiated through her bones as the breath rushed out of her lungs. The phone flew from her hand and spun down the hallway. Standing above her, the man raised his arm. Something was in his hand. Was he holding a gun?

Henry stepped out of his truck, fighting against the desire to stop and stretch. He'd already spent more hours than he'd like in the front seat of his truck, and his spine had lodged a formal complaint. He'd nodded off and woken many times, but he thought he'd just seen the strobe of a flashlight from the men's side of the employee lodging. It was possible one of the college kids was sneaking back in through a window, like some of the guys had done to avoid curfew when he'd spent his time guiding. Given that Nora had witnessed a shooter, he needed to know she was okay. A quick look through the front window should be enough. He strode to the front door.

He spotted a shadowed figure standing over Nora. The man dropped into a lunge with the gun raised in the air, reaching for Nora's neck as if he was going to smack her hard with the weapon. "No!"

Henry pulled at the front door, willing to shoot out the front door window to get inside, but the door swung open easily. The man spun and rushed at Henry. "Drop your weapon," Henry shouted, reaching for his holster. The figure barreled right into his stomach, using the gun to hit Henry's elbow.

Henry's eyes rolled back as he growled, absorbing the pain of the hard impact on a sensitive joint. He blinked rapidly as the man ran past him into the night.

"Nora," he croaked. "Are you okay?"

"Go." Her voice shook but sounded strong enough. He pushed off on his heel, sprinting after the man who'd run into the space between the rafting office and lodging. Henry's arm throbbed but he grit his teeth and all-out sprinted.

The man, dressed in a dark turtleneck and pants, looked over his shoulder, only his eyes visible behind the ski mask. Twenty feet away. The man took a sharp turn into the campfire area. Henry pumped his legs faster and hurdled over one of the logs used as a bench. The man disappeared into the tree line. Henry grabbed his flashlight with his left hand and searched the trees.

Five frustrating minutes passed and he couldn't find any sign of the man. Nothing. He balled up his fists and stomped the ground. He'd be foolish to run into the forest without any backup or visibility with a gunman on the loose.

He took out his phone and called Dispatch as he jogged back to the lodge. Several rooms now had lights on as well as the hallway. The front door had been left open and Bobby Olson, a guide Henry knew as being a friend to Nora's family, stepped onto the threshold. "Are you okay? Nora said the man hit you with his gun."

"I wasn't shot, so I'll be fine." Nora might still need an ambulance. "Where's Nora?"

Her door opened and she appeared, wearing a pair of green-and-purple-plaid pajamas.

"I'm fine." She placed an ice pack on the back of her head. She looked pointedly at Bobby. "I really am. Could you tell the guides everything is okay and turn off the hallway light so they can get a little more sleep? It's not quite time to start breakfast."

"Sheriff's been contacted," Henry said. "Do you need an ambulance?"

"No, I just hit the floor hard. I think it might've been much worse if you hadn't showed up." She smiled shyly. "Thank you." She spun around, stepping inside her room in the direction he remembered was the kitchen. She stepped back out with another ice pack, arm outstretched. "Do *you* need an ambulance?"

Bobby looked between them both and nodded. "Looks like the two of you have each other's backs. G'night." He sauntered off.

Henry accepted the ice pack and placed it on his already swelling elbow. "I'll be fine."

The hallway light went off, leaving them bathed with only the light from Nora's room and the lights from the shared bathrooms, which Bobby had decided to leave on. "The front door was open."

"I figured that out when you came in. Bobby is sure he locked it, though, and I believe him. He's my right-hand man." Her eyes widened. "Why were *you* here?"

He shrugged. "In the area. I think it's time I took a look in Dexter's room. Can you show me which one?"

The sound of crunching gravel drew their attention through the front door in time to see Deputy Zach O'Brien park. Henry propped open the door and beckoned for Zach to come inside.

Nora groaned. "Why'd it have to be him?"

"You don't like him?"

"Is he going to try to tell me Dexter's death was a suicide?"

"His wife is taking over Frank's bistro in town. Restaurants are always a risky business, but I'm sure you can understand the deputy's fear about the tourist season being diminished in some way."

"Oh."

Her eyes were downcast, and he wondered if she was thinking about Maya. A few years ago, it had been her sister who was supposed to take over the bistro. "Any, uh, word from your sister?" He told himself he was asking to keep her mind off the intruder.

"No. She said her reputation was ruined here forever." The steely tone returned to her voice, and he knew she still blamed him for her sister leaving town. "I get a text or email occasionally on holidays," she added softly.

"That's good." The awkwardness between them seemed to heighten. Simply being in the lodge hit Henry over the head with memories. He'd first proposed in this hallway, on impulse, without a ring or a plan, before he'd left for training.

But a couple of years later, after he'd returned, he'd also told Nora, in this same hallway, that he needed to take her to the sheriff's office for questioning. As a new law enforcement ranger, he might have been a little too eager to prove himself. He'd come to pick Nora up for an early dinner, a few months after moving back. Her door was open, as it often was during the day so guides could find her easily. But that day, he'd found her holding a giant package of white powder, about to hand it over to her sister.

At the time, Henry had suspected Maya had been going down the wrong path for a while. He'd made a knee-jerk decision and taken both Maya and Nora to the sheriff. The white powder had turned out to be lidocaine, an ingredient often used in over-the-counter burn creams. Maya claimed she'd been trying to invent a pain-reliever for sunburned rafting guides. Nora had been in the process of confronting Maya when he'd found them. But, unlike Henry, Nora had believed Maya's explanation. Henry knew lidocaine was often used to cut drugs, but possession wasn't enough to make an arrest stick. That night, Maya had grabbed her stuff and left town, despite Nora's heartbroken pleas.

That night had been the beginning of the end to their

relationship, though he still maintained it wasn't the main reason for their breakup. They'd been drifting apart long before that.

Zach reached the entrance, and Henry's trip down memory lane halted. Nora walked in front of the two men and gestured at Dexter's room. Zach put on gloves and opened the door. "Unlocked."

"It was locked before I went to bed. I checked," she said.

The door swung open, revealing a flipped-over mattress, emptied-out dresser and desk, and an open trunk at the foot of the bed. Ransacked. Zach glanced at Henry over his shoulder. "Last night, Deputy Alexander interviewed some of the guides about Dexter." He gave a nod in Nora's direction. "The guides say he was bragging about having a lot of cash. This could've been a break-in for the money."

"But I heard Dexter say he had something that the gunman wanted."

Zach raised his eyebrows. "Please wait in the hallway, miss."

Henry's ire rose. He didn't like anyone dismissing Nora, even if they did need to consider all possibilities. Voicing his concern wouldn't do him any favors. Working with the County Sheriff's Department and the Forest Service was a constant game of politics and knowing when to keep his mouth shut.

He didn't want to give anyone any reason to kick him off the case. Especially since late last night the deputy had the audacity to suggest that Nora being shot at was just Dexter trying to warn her off from interfering with his suicide. An unlikely scenario, but Perry Fletcher hadn't discouraged the theory.

Zach walked forward and fingered through the open chest of clothes, water guns, video games and controllers. He held up a piece of paper. "Looks like we have a suicide note."

Nora gasped from the hallway. "The intruder probably planted it."

Zach raised an eyebrow but said nothing.

Henry wasn't wearing gloves, so he looked over Zach's shoulder and examined the note. "'I've tried but I can't take it anymore. Please tell my family I'm sorry,'" he read aloud.

Nora shook her head. "No. Definitely not. That doesn't sound like him at all." Her eyes widened. "He wasn't even done with his training and he was already causing trouble and bragging about his future. I have his handwritten application still in the office. You can compare the handwriting. I'm sure you'll see it's a fake." By her eager tone Henry could tell she was confident it would be the proof they needed to totally dismiss the suicide theory.

She beckoned them to follow.

Zach pulled an evidence bag from his pocket and slipped the notepad-size paper into the bag. Closing the door, he muttered something about fingerprints.

"The intruder wore gloves," Henry said. "But maybe one of the guides knew Dexter well enough to tell if something was missing from his room."

The horizon to the east lit the mountains with a dazzling array of orange and pink hues as they hustled across the dirt covered in pine needles to the company office. Once inside, Nora found a key in a drawer and hastily opened a filing cabinet.

She grumbled under her breath as she pulled out numerous manila files until she waved a crumpled form. "Found it." She studied the paper herself before begrudgingly placing it on the customer counter. Henry and Zach compared the two samples. He wasn't a handwriting analyst, but unless they were dealing with an excellent forger, the writing seemed to be an exact match.

He felt Nora lean over his shoulder, studying the form alongside.

Zach's phone rang. He took it out and relayed to whomever was on the other end of the line that they'd found a suicide note. Henry strained to hear what sounded like talk about a gun. Zach answered in the affirmative and signed off. "Carl said the manager of Sauvage Outdoor finally answered his call. He says Dexter came in a few days ago to buy a gun. My guess is Perry will have what he needs to close the case now."

Nora spun on her heel and stormed out of the office. Henry rushed after her. "Nora, stop. Please."

She turned toward him, the wind blowing back her hair. Judging by the storm in her eyes, he knew they couldn't face the present before they confronted the past. Again.

FOUR

Nora breathed deeply in and out, trying to slow her heart rate. She steeled herself as best she could against what Henry might say.

"I believe you," he said softly. "One hundred percent." He stepped closer. "But I'm only on this case because I'm invited to do so. I need to be strategic."

Her forehead tightened. Words. They were just words. She'd thought before that he'd had her back only to be proven wrong in the most humiliating way. "I still have a business to run." And save, hopefully, but she didn't need Henry's pity. "I'm going to get ready and prep the other rafting sites." She held up a hand. "Don't worry. I'll avoid the crime scene."

"I was actually hoping you'd be willing to take me to the crime scene."

"Why?"

"Perry indicated last night that he would be willing to take a second look once I explained that our witness had been shot at. I don't think Zach knows what he's talking about back there, but I would like to find evidence to back up your testimony." His eyebrows jumped and he held out an open hand. "I have other options, but as you know, you're the best and this would get you back on the river faster."

She should be grateful, but for reasons she didn't fully understand herself, her blood only pumped hotter. "Fine, but you're going to have to come along to at least another site or two before I'm done for the day. I need to keep site preps moving before early season starts. Be at the dock in thirty minutes." She spun on her heel and strode back to her room.

She yanked open the top dresser drawer to grab her clothes and her fingers caught on the familiar outline of the silver frame. The photo had been there for so long, she'd ignored its existence as if it were part of the drawer itself. Her fingers wrapped around the frame and slowly slid it out from under the extensive collection of wool socks.

Henry's smiling face beamed up through the frame's glass. His arm was wrapped around Nora's shoulders as they sat side by side in a camp chair made for two, in front of a roaring campfire. They'd both changed so much since then, but something about the photo—maybe the reminder of happier times—had kept her from ever getting rid of it. And now she was about to spend time with him again. She glanced up at the only other framed photo still on the dresser. The one of her mother, her sister and her, right before Mom had passed away the day after Nora's fifteenth birthday.

Family always came first, and while Henry had nothing to do with her mom's passing, he had everything to do with her sister's disappearance from her life. She still had no idea where Maya was now. It'd been six months since a postcard, the last one coming from Seattle with a bogus return address.

Nora shoved the framed photo back underneath the socks. No time for a memory show. She prepped for a day on the river and, true to her word, found Henry on the dock thirty minutes later.

"Perry said he's about to drop in the water at the Savage bridge."

She nodded. Locals often used the "Savage" nickname for all things Sauvage. Perhaps to make it sound more American. In the same way Boise had been named, French fur trappers had named the Sauvage River, meaning "wild." Now the nickname seemed more a reminder of Tommy's and Dexter's murders.

She handed Henry a microwaved burrito. "You might want some breakfast before we hit the rapids."

His eyes widened. "That was thoughtful. Thank you."

"You might not be thanking me later. I'm taking the fastest currents all the way there. You shouldn't need to paddle, though." She might've imagined it, but he seemed to have paled. She remembered the long months he'd spent in a cast after his rafting accident, but he'd never talked about it.

"Of course," he said with a nod. "Fastest is best." They hit the water a few minutes later.

Trying to keep Henry from needing to paddle, she was able to block out her emotions and focus on the currents. The sounds of cheerful birds and leaves rustling against each other almost made her forget why they were on the water in the first place.

She missed interacting with guests on the water, observing the way families bonded, and the wide-eyed wonder and gasps from children. Once the rafting season began, she was responsible for managing the business from the office and would only have time to get back on the river if there was a problem. Problems always meant someone was hurt, missing, or worse. She fervently prayed every night that there would be no problems.

They rounded the bend and she guided the raft toward the beach. Perry, already standing on the sand, helped to drag the raft farther up on land before they stepped out. The dark circles under his eyes seemed to age the man ten years, but Nora found it hard to feel sorry for him when he'd challenged what she'd seen yesterday. "I have bad news," he said. He hitched a thumb over his shoulder.

The picnic area looked trashed. Smoke tendrils drifted in the air from the used firepit. Wrappers and debris seemed to be everywhere. Henry groaned aloud. "Teens?"

"If I had to guess." Perry shifted uncomfortably to talk to Nora. "Henry reminded me you interned once as river patrol. Thanks for helping out again when we're short on resources, but I need to remind you not to touch anything."

Nora steeled her features, trying not to show surprise. Her time as a river patrol guide was really about educating people about the rules of the river, checking for fishing and rafting permits, and cleaning up trash. She loved every minute of those months, but she never took part in any investigations or law enforcement. While Perry hadn't apologized for his quick dismissal last night, she knew him enough to know that his soft tone meant he'd changed his mind and was taking her seriously now.

Everyone knew the rangers were stretched thin. So why was it easier for her to forgive Perry for his mistake than Henry when he tried to arrest her sister?

"Where were you shot at?" Henry asked.

Nora pointed along the shore. "I ran from my boat to behind those boulders. Sorry I can't be more exact. I was focused on getting to safety."

Henry's neck reddened, the way it did when he was upset. Perry scratched his chin before he spoke. "The waves might've already lapped up what we're looking for." Perry and Henry turned away, talking in low tones. They split up, gloves on their hands and evidence bags in their pockets.

She wanted to be wrong about the murder so they could still use Sandy Cape for rafting. So her aunt's business wouldn't deteriorate. So the economy and livelihoods of the townspeople wouldn't suffer. But yet, she also wanted proof that she hadn't been imagining things.

Wanting to know, her own mind won out. Nora ducked underneath the crime scene tape stretched between two of the boulders near the picnic table. She had no interest in revisiting the area where Dexter had been murdered just beyond the tree line—Henry and Perry could deal with that. But she knew the townspeople and teens in the area well enough that she wondered if there might be a clue as to who had ruined the crime scene.

A box of store-bought brownies was open and left on the ground. Except, there wasn't a single frosted brownie missing. Odd. Wouldn't teenagers want to devour that? The picnic table would need dousing with several tubs of water to remove the sticky traces of something maroon. She followed the trail and found a half-empty box of raspberry-filled donuts. And next to it, on the ground beside the firepit, lay a package of unwrapped, smoked salmon. It was still whole, as if someone had dumped the fish on the sandy ground. Most teenagers didn't have the kind of money to be buying smoked salmon.

A pile of uneaten hot dogs rested next to the firewood. Nora stared at the scene, her eyes drifting to another hot dog, half eaten, about a half a foot away. So, if a group of teens had brought all this food, had something scared them away before they could enjoy it? She scratched her head. That didn't really make sense, but it was actually more dangerous that they'd left out all the food.

The Sauvage tied with the Salmon River as the second deepest river gorge in North America. To protect both the area and to keep everyone safe, visitors knew to pack everything in and out so as not to attract wild animals to sites like this. The spread seemed almost like the perfect meal plan if you wanted to lure a...

Her mouth dried up as her eyes drifted back to the raspberry-filled donuts. The box looked as if it'd been dragged then left behind. Right next to the discarded box was a dusty footprint, barely discernable in the sand. Her eyes darted to the hot dogs. Three feet away, the sand mixed with mud and revealed another half a footprint. Something that most definitely had long claws.

"Henry?" She called out and looked over her shoulder to see him balancing precariously on top of one of the boulders, near where she'd hidden from the bullets.

He didn't look up. His eyebrows were low, so intense was his focus on something roughly five feet from him.

"I'm afraid we might have some wildlife nearby," she said, even louder. She looked around to find Perry, but it was as if the man had disappeared. She should grab a trash bag and clean the food up immediately, but she would need Perry's permission first.

She stepped forward, following the tracks. A small cry that sounded almost like an exotic bird with a little guttural growl at the end sent chills up her spine. She squinted and, past the thick foliage, two sets of eyes peered back at her. With the softest-looking black fur, two cubs fought to climb over a fallen log. Their limbs appeared too big for their small bodies, and they stumbled over each other. If she had to guess, they looked to be roughly three months old. "Henry?" she called out again, keeping her voice friendly but loud. "I *really* need your attention."

Because where there were cubs, there was often—

"Yeah, I'll be there in one minute." Henry held up one hand but didn't look away from the object of his focus. Willing his eyes to zoom wasn't working, but there was something reflective on the top edge of one of the small rocks. For all he knew, it could be a wrapper, but his gut told him it might be a bullet casing. If it turned out to be a match for the type of bullet used on Dexter, Perry would have no choice but to sound the alarm they had a murderer on the loose. And maybe, just maybe, they'd finally get another lead to solving Tommy's Sorenson's murder.

Trying to reach the item was proving precarious, as it was just beyond the highest boulder. The way the sun shone on the slick rocks, everything looked shiny. He was afraid if he glanced away for even a second, it would take him forever to find it again.

"Henry!"

His gaze darted to Nora. Her arms were high in the air, but there'd been no mistaking the alarm in her shout. A giant paw snapped the branches of a bush fifteen feet in front of her. The snout poked out first, followed by a loud huff. A black bear, at least six feet long, stepped out into the open picnic area and slapped the ground with its paw. Its ears stood straight up, then flattened as its head ducked down, scared but ready to fight.

"Hey!" Henry yelled. "Get out of here." He slipped down the boulder and felt a sharp edge rip his knee open.

"She has cubs," Nora said loudly, waving her arms.

The bear took one step forward and began clacking its teeth together. Four fast clicks followed by a growl. The enormous animal turned away and Henry almost breathed a sigh of relief until the mama bear spun back around, taking another closer step to Nora, huffing and releasing another rendition of the odd chattering sound.

Normally when dealing with a black bear, the procedure was to make yourself big and stand your ground, but when cubs were involved, the usually timid animal's behavior could transition to something unpredictable. Henry slid all the way down to the ground, taking the scratches with inward groans. He picked up a stick of driftwood and stepped away from the boulders, then waved the stick in the air. "Hey!"

The bear shifted her gaze from Nora to Henry and huffed again. She picked up the box of brownies with her jaw then turned and jogged toward the boulders, uttering a repetitive grunt that sounded like she was ordering her cubs "Off! Off!" The cubs barreled after her, tripping occasionally and scrambling over the rocks. The mama stopped every few steps to look over her shoulder, keeping a keen eye on Henry and Nora.

Henry stood tall, his stick still in the air, but he didn't want to spook the mama into acting aggressively. The cubs moved along, across the boulders he'd just slid down. At the far edge of the pile, they disappeared into the tree line closest to the river rapids.

Nora dropped her hands to her knees, leaning over and breathing deeply. "Wow." She half laughed, but the way her voice wobbled could easily be mistaken for a cry. "I love black bears," she said. "They're beautiful, but I kept thinking that I was in the way of them enjoying these snacks." She waved at the spread of food in front of her. "At least she had good taste taking the brownies with her. I don't think they'd been touched yet."

Henry finally lowered the branch he'd been holding. A mama bear, he knew, could run thirty miles an hour, but he finally felt confident that if she decided to turn around now, they'd have time to prepare. "Where's Perry?"

"I don't know. It's like he disappeared."

Henry grabbed his radio and sent a call out to Perry. No reply.

Nora pointed in front of her. "Take a good look at all the food that was left here by the supposed partygoers."

"It's like the perfect storm of bear attractants."

"Maybe it was meant to be a bear party."

The idea seemed ludicrous. As he studied the grounds, he had to admit the entire crime scene had been ruined. All the sand had been shifted. Branches and foliage had been trampled and...

Henry spun around to the boulders. He struggled to climb back up the slimy rocks as his knee, the side of his leg and his hands stung from his earlier quick descent. No matter which way he turned his head, adjusted his body and squinted, he'd lost sight of the metallic reflection he'd spotted earlier. He balanced on his good knee and grabbed his flashlight. Maybe the beam would catch the reflection if the casing had fallen in a crack.

The cubs had tripped right over this particular boulder. If one of their clumsy paws had hit it, the likely trajectory would be the river. The way the water aerated here, it would pull the bullet casing into the current and toss it around the rapids before allowing it to sink to the bottom.

"Pretty sure the sun is out." Perry's deep voice sounded like a Southern drawl when he was joking around. "No need for a flashlight."

Henry didn't bother to explain himself and kept the flashlight steady, hunting. "Where have you been?" His beam found nothing.

"Are you serious? I was looking—"

"He tried calling you on the radio," Nora said, her voice soft. "There were bears here. A mama and two cubs."

"And I had possible evidence up here that's gone now." Henry clicked off the light and made his way back down the boulders.

Perry took off his green hat and rubbed his wrinkled brow. "We'll need to get a ranger to start tracking the bears, then. Make sure they're maintaining distance from people." He gave Nora a side glance. "I need a moment alone to discuss the case with Henry."

She pursed her lips and gave Henry a meaningful look. He had no idea what she was trying to communicate by the subtle widening of her eyes, but she obviously didn't appreciate being excluded. She went back to the raft and waited.

"Now, can you tell me where you went?" Henry asked.

"I was deeper in the woods. I must've lost my signal, but you can handle a few black bears on your own." Perry's eyes shifted, downcast. "I went back behind the trees to check my ATV tracks from the other night.

You were, uh…" He cleared his throat. "Right that I should've been watching. I'd just come from a meth lab complete with booby traps, and I wasn't in the best state of mind."

Henry shook his head as if the thought no longer needed to be considered. They were all human, unfortunately, and the strain of being understaffed at all times was a burden they all did their best to carry.

Perry pointed to the south. "I found another set of tracks. It's not an ATV, but maybe a dirt bike. I lost the tracks in the foliage, but they seemed to point in the direction of the Englemann ranch. You know how they have signs about private property everywhere."

Henry's shoulders somewhat relaxed now that Perry was beginning to see reason. "He wouldn't take kindly to trespassers. Someone needs to talk to him."

"Exactly. I'll go there and interview him as soon as we wrap up here."

"Are you ready to consider that Dexter was murdered?"

Perry's forehead creased. "I'm ready to take Nora's testimony a whole lot more seriously. But it also means someone intentionally tried to discredit her given the way the scene was set."

"Maybe they intended to make it look like a suicide from the beginning and didn't want to veer off the plan." Henry pointed at the trashed scene. "Speaking of which, could this have been done on purpose? Given our high bear population out here, all this food seems straight out of—"

"A black bear cafeteria," Perry interjected, putting

his green cap back on and adjusting it. "I'd rather not have it public knowledge we're considering suspicious death yet." He folded his arms across his chest. "We announced it immediately with Tommy and look where that got us. A media circus and it still took the FBI days to get down here. I'd rather let the shooter think he got away with it and see if he makes mistakes. At least until I get the ballistics report. Then we take it public. In the meantime," he said as he started to walk away, "we investigate all angles."

Henry knew Perry well enough to know when he'd given his final word.

Nora had dragged the raft to a place they could easily push off into the water. She turned to him as he approached and opened her mouth as if to ask a question, then closed it.

"I meant it before when I said I believed you," he said. "Perry does, as well."

Her eyebrows rose and fell in a heartbeat. "He has a funny way of showing it. A bit dodgy, really."

"I need to stay on the case," Henry said. "We just need to keep our eyes wide open." His gut told him that he could no longer trust his mentor. He couldn't share the battle with Nora, though. The sensation felt uncomfortably familiar. His distrust in Nora all those years ago had also been a gut reaction. His instincts had served him well for many years except in that one moment, but if he couldn't trust his gut, then what did he have left?

FIVE

The tension between Henry and Nora continued to build as Deputy Carl Alexander drove them back to The Sauvage Run. Carl remained silent while he drove, a welcome change after Zach O'Brien's talkative nature yesterday. He dropped them off in the lodge parking lot, turned around and drove off.

Uncle Frank, in his designer navy-and-white-striped shirt, jeans and Birkenstocks, stood next to the rafting shed, talking to Bobby and her second most loyal rafting guide, Lizzie Hartman. *Ex* Uncle Frank, she corrected herself.

No one could deny Frank Milner was a youthful fifty-five-year-old. Somehow his tanned skin didn't age him. He covered up the gray in his dark hair, though he claimed he was still naturally young. Nora'd found the dye kit once when he'd stayed in the apartment over the office with Aunt Linda.

The women apparently fell for his smooth lines given his philandering ways, but he had the reputation as a hard worker who invested any profits he made right back into the town. He owned multiple businesses, like the bistro, the outdoor store and the competing rafting company. It was probably the reason people had voted for him as county commissioner, as well. He had a vested interest in seeing the tourism industry succeed.

Though, for some reason, Aunt Linda had wanted to keep their businesses separate. Maybe she'd always had an inkling the marriage wouldn't last.

Bobby and Lizzie caught sight of Nora and waved before they hustled away.

"Would you like me to stay?" Henry asked softly.

"I'm fine. Go get some rest." If he'd asked a few years ago, she would've taken him up on his offer.

"I'll be in touch," he said with a nod before he got into his truck and drove away.

Uncle Frank, she'd noticed, had watched the interchange before he approached.

Nora lifted the raft over her shoulder and made her way to the shed. "Commissioner Milner," she said with a nod.

He raised an eyebrow, maybe a little surprised she'd chosen to stop calling him "uncle," but his face smoothed into that charming smile. "How are you, Nora?"

She unlocked the padlock with one hand and maneuvered the unruly raft back into its holding place. "I'm fine, thank you."

"I know your aunt would want me to make sure you were all right, especially considering…"

"She'd want you to try to poach our employees?" She closed and locked the shed with a little more force. In that instance, she knew. "You're the one who contacted the magazine and told them not to come." Dexter's passing hadn't been featured in any news media yet. But someone had let the magazine know the minute it had happened, otherwise she wouldn't have gotten the email mere hours afterward.

Frank shrugged. "Word travels fast in a small town. You may not believe me, but I'm working in your aunt's best interests. If the magazine feature is unfavorable, it negatively impacts my rafting company, too. We're the only two companies on this river. Better not risk them coming than to find you not at your best." He gestured at her as if to prove his point.

"Thanks for the concern," she quipped. "Now, if you'll excuse me, I'm going to go see if I still have a staff left—"

"When will Linda be coming home? It might be time to consider consolidation." He gestured behind him at the rafting office. "I'm willing to take this off her hands."

Nora fought back a snarky response. If her aunt had refused to consolidate the companies during their marriage, why would he think she would do it now? What her aunt did or didn't do wasn't his business anymore, but at the same time, Nora didn't want to hinder Aunt Linda's healing process by fanning the flames of animosity. "I can't be the middleman, here," she said instead.

Frank leaned back ever so slightly and looked around as if she'd just told him the weather forecast. "Well, if she asks, my offer to help is genuine." He strolled off to where he'd parked his Range Rover.

Nora's insides felt like they were vibrating. She purposefully dropped her shoulders to their normal place and went back to her room to change before spending the rest of the day helping Bobby train the staff. The office cell phone rang. "The Sauvage Run, this is Nora speaking. How may I help you?"

"Hi, Nora. This is Angela Johnson from *Wonder Travel Magazine*. I sent you an email but—"

"I'm sorry. I haven't had a chance to read it, but I can assure you we're still on target for our early season run." Sauvage Run needed enough visitors to use the permits they'd bought from the forest service, or Nora had no idea how her aunt would stay afloat this year without selling the business. Aside from the small apartment they'd lived in before her mom's passing, the rafting company was the only home Nora had ever known. Where would she go? And if Maya ever came back, how would they find each other?

"We had an anonymous—"

"Our competitor admitted he gave you that anonymous tip." She steeled her nerves. This was the last chance to make her aunt's business stay afloat. She had to make it work. "We did have an unfortunate death here, but I assure you our rafting guides will be ready to give our visitors the time of their lives when the season starts." Nora blinked back a wave of desperation.

"Sounds good. That's why we always confirm our sources," Angela said with a laugh. "If anything changes, let me know. Oh, and the other reason I called is that our photographer is coming with me."

"Perfect. We'll see you soon." Nora ended the call and lifted her face to the sky. Everything needed to start going smoothly. Now. "Please help," she prayed in a whisper.

She worked all afternoon in the office, already two days behind in the prep work she needed to do. Tomorrow morning, she would hit the fastest currents and prepare all the other sites. She would have to keep a lookout for somewhere besides Sandy Cape for the guides to stop to prepare a lunch break for their rafting guests or, possibly, locate a completely different launch point. She studied maps and made note of potential new break points. The ideas were theoretical at best until she could get on the river to see what the high snowmelt had done. She jotted down a note where Perry had warned her of a mountainous boulder before the final take-out location.

By the time she joined her staff at the campground for dinner, Bobby and Lizzie seemed to be avoiding her pointed gaze. Today, the trainees had learned how to make grilled salmon, salad, and sliced apples for a gourmet dinner. One of the reasons Frank had likely wanted to recruit Bobby was for his renowned cooking and teaching skills. And Lizzie, only seven years older than Nora, was in her late thirties and had been a rafting guide for almost twenty years. Besides Maya and Aunt Linda, those two employees were the closest Nora had to family. Had they finally agreed to let Frank steal them away?

"We said no," Lizzie said as she handed Nora a paper plate and sat next to her. "But he's getting harder to resist with the promised increase in pay."

"You know I would match it if I could."

"I know, which is why I keep saying no." Lizzie smiled. "Besides, it seemed obvious he was really there to talk to Bobby more than me."

Bobby joined them. He looked over his shoulder. "I kept Frank from talking to the guides, Nora, but it's only a matter of time. Some of these guys are townies and have connections to Frank's employees. They get back to their cell phones and internet in the lodge at night and they'll eventually find out they can make more money at Frank's."

The salmon no longer melted in her mouth. She forced herself to smile and make conversation about training. At the end of the week, she would be the trainees' final instructor with a full day on the river, testing their swift water rescue techniques. If the students and Bobby had done their jobs well, the day on the river would be more exhilarating than scary.

Once darkness enveloped the campground, she left the lesson on fireside Dutch Oven pineapple upside-down cake to the professionals. She'd never been a fan of pineapple anyway. Always made her tongue itch. She made her way back to the lodge but slowed as she noticed the moonlit shape of a vehicle at the far edge of the parking lot. The outline of a person shifted in the front window.

Someone was watching her.

Henry gritted his teeth together. Nora shouldn't be out at night. He thought she'd be safely inside the lodge by now. Maybe she wouldn't notice that he was sitting inside the truck. Her hair was loose, something she only allowed in evenings when she was no longer expected to help customers or be on the river. The breeze blew the dark strands from her face as she squinted into the night in his direction. She turned on her heel and entered the employee quarters.

He blew out a breath. If she had noticed him, she wouldn't have let his presence go without comment. On one hand, this meant he didn't need to explain why he planned to sleep in the parking lot until the case was solved, namely that he still cared and worried about her.

He exhaled. Even now, his fingers itched to dial her on the phone. She should've instantly reported a vehicle in the parking lot. He clicked his radio volume a tick louder in case she actually did call the dispatcher. He strained his eyes toward the employee lodge, willing his vision to see farther than natural into the darkness. Maybe he'd see Nora's light flick on behind the blinds, and know she was safe for the night.

Floodlights burst on from four points of the lodge. He reared back, eyes squeezed shut, and elbowed the console. The sharp plastic edge scratched his arm. "Aw, come on!" His seat vibrated. He looked around, blinking rapidly, and hoped the bright white spots would go away sooner than later so he could find his phone, which had slipped between the seat and the console. His fingers strained through the narrow space, wiggled the phone back out and answered the call, his breath heavy.

"Did anyone ever tell you it's impolite to spy?" Nora asked.

Henry placed a hand over his closed eyes. "Did anyone ever tell you it's impolite to blind an officer of the law with floodlights? Any chance you could turn those back off now? They must be brighter than the sun."

A knock on his window made him flinch. He twisted

to find Nora standing at the driver's-side door. She pressed her lips together, but couldn't conceal her amusement from him. He clicked off the phone and rolled down his window. "Okay, you caught me. But I was just—"

"Doing your job. Yes, I knew you would say that, but it would've been nice if you had let me know first." She gestured with her chin at the thick blanket and pillow in her arms. "You could either make sure I'm safe from the confines of your uncomfortable truck or do the same thing in an empty room across the hall from me." Her eyes widened and her forehead creased. "You're bleeding, Henry. In two places."

He glanced down. His elbow had the slightest cut and his knee wound had reopened from the nasty jab it'd endured on the boulders. He'd meant to bandage it up after dinner and a shower, but it had stopped bleeding at the time and he'd forgotten. "It'll be fine."

"At least come inside and wash the cuts properly."

He was about to point out that he was a ranger with an amazing first-aid kit in the back when a scent wafted through the open window. He closed his eyes and inhaled appreciatively. "Bobby's cooking?"

"Training the cooks tonight. Upside-down pineapple cake. I'm sure he'd be willing to give you my piece in exchange for ensuring him a good night's sleep."

"I don't know how you can dislike—"

"Heated pineapple is the worst. Shouldn't be part of dessert or pizza."

He fought not to laugh. She only got this worked up when she'd reached the point of exhaustion, which meant next she would either be laughing hysterically or crying. He really didn't want to push her past the point of no return.

She shifted onto one leg, her other hip jutting out. "Anyway, the point is, do we have a deal?"

"Like I said it's just—"

"Your job." Her lips twitched to the side. "Henry, we both know you aren't doing this as official business, but I…" She took a deep breath and her eyes softened. "I appreciate it. So why don't you help ease my guilt and sleep with one ear open on a real mattress?"

His back reminded him of all the muscles that were still angry with him due to last night's ill attempt at sleeping in the truck. "Well, I could take a small break for cake, I suppose." He reached to open the door. "But there's no need for guilt." Nora cared about everyone, almost to a fault. She hadn't yet learned that being vulnerable only gave people the upper hand. Whether they took advantage of it or not, they had power. Ironically, she was one of the people that had taught him that hard lesson.

"Think of it this way. You might've caught the intruder if you were closer last night."

Despite her monotone, he caught the tiniest bit of a wobble in her voice. "You knew I was out here?"

"I put two and two together this morning."

"I'm sorry I didn't catch the guy."

"You stopped him from hurting me." She flashed him a wary smile as they walked side by side across the lot.

"So I take it Frank wanted a chat." He pulled his shoulders back. In the past, she'd vent, he'd give advice, she'd let him know she just wanted him to listen, and he'd fire back that what she really wanted was him to produce chocolate on the spot—which he usually surprised her by doing. Oh, how he'd loved surprising her. She had a special smile reserved for only those moments. A smile he couldn't help but kiss. The memory caused his heart to squeeze with pain. He shouldn't have even asked her about Frank. He needed to do a better job at keeping interactions related only to the case.

She opened her mouth as if to spill the beans but then clamped it shut and walked inside the lodge. "Nothing I can't handle, thanks." The front door of the employee lodge was not locked during the day, which was part of the reason Henry wanted to stay nearby.

She unlocked the room across the hall from hers. The space wasn't as nice as Nora's apartment, but all the furniture and linens appeared to be clean. She disappeared across the hall and returned with two bandages. "Unicorns on rainbows? Or construction equipment?"

"Rainbows," he answered on instinct. The choices weren't a surprise; everything about a rafting guide's appearance had to be fun, even their bandages.

He sat on the edge of the mattress. She sat in the chair opposite and leaned forward, intent on studying his cut knee. For a second, he was ready to let her tend his wounds—scratches, really—just to get closer. The realization disturbed him to his core. Would they have been able to get over their differences if he had handled that one night better?

Bobby appeared over her shoulder. "I got an urgent text for cake?" He lifted a paper plate with the largest slice of pineapple upside-down cake Henry had ever seen.

"I'm pretty sure the cake will help you more than these could." Nora laughed, shoved the bandages at Henry, and made to leave the room, patting Bobby on the shoulder as she made her way past him.

Bobby beamed. "I'm glad you recruited him. You two are great at teamwork. I wasn't happy about you prepping the sites alone tomorrow."

Nora turned to Bobby, her face devoid of expression. "I didn't recruit him."

Henry's gut twisted. She had planned to get back on the river first thing in the morning without him and prep all the sites herself? He could see it as plain as day in her face.

She whirled around as if ready to defend an argument he had yet to present. "Consider it as volunteering for river patrol—"

He shot to his feet. "That's an excuse if I ever heard one. You were going to go out alone? When there's—"

"Tell me this." Her eyes flashed as she stepped closer to look him straight in the eyes. "Do you trust Perry?"

"I think the more important question is do you trust me?" The muscles behind his shoulder blades tightened the more he thought about the insinuation. He didn't need Nora to tell him how to do his job.

"How can you trust someone who doesn't trust you back?" She blinked rapidly. "Thank you for bringing the cake, Bobby." Her voice warbled ever so slightly. "Good night." She dashed across the hall, closing her door before Henry could formulate a response.

Bobby's jaw couldn't have dropped any lower. He placed the plate on the dresser and stepped back, hands up, as if it, too, might become as explosive as Nora and Henry's conversation. "I obviously made an assumption." He shook his head. "Sorry."

"No, I'm the one who should apologize."

He nodded. "Yep. But not to me, and not about this." Bobby sighed. "Look, man. It's none of my business, but my nose is already stuck in far enough to know that you two are better together than apart."

You're right. It's none of your business. Henry scratched his head and fought to keep the thought from flying out of his mouth.

Bobby stepped out of the room with a wave. "Good night, Henry."

Except it wouldn't be a good night. Henry had no guarantees he could keep Nora safe if she wasn't willing to share her thoughts and plans with him. Her lack of trust in him was like a sucker punch, taking his appetite away even when the tantalizing scent of pineapple filled the room. He closed the door partially, using the desk chair to prop it open a fraction to better keep an ear out.

Actions brought results. So he would do whatever he needed to do to find the killer in record time, for both Tommy's and Nora's sake. He grabbed the piece of cake as if it were a slice of pizza and shoved a sizeable bite into his mouth even though at the moment his mouth refused to register any taste.

If he didn't succeed, he feared his own heart was in grave danger.

SIX

Nora peeked out of her room to make sure no one was in the hallway before she left the lodge.

It was barely seven in the morning, and none of her employees stirred until sunrise, closer to eight at this time of year. She hitched the pack on her shoulder, still bristling over the exchange from the previous night, and made her way to the raft shed to grab her kayak.

"That better be for two," a male voice said. A shadow moved from the space between the lodge and the shed, and her breath hitched.

She grabbed the pepper spray, hanging from a loop on her wrist, and flicked the lever to Armed. The shadow moved into the light, hands raised. Henry's eyes flashed. "I've been trained to endure it but please don't. It gives me a headache for, like, a week."

She exhaled and lowered her arm. "You scared me!"

"That wasn't my intention. I thought you would recognize my voice."

Her chest tightened at the gap between what they used to be and what they were now. "You don't usually sound so—"

"I haven't had enough coffee. I really didn't mean to scare you, but the point is I'm not letting you go on the river alone with a potential killer on the loose. Honestly, I don't think you should be going out at all."

She turned back to the oars. "I don't have a choice. This place feeds too many mouths. Aunt Linda is counting on me and…" She didn't want to voice her last reason. If she didn't keep the rafting company open, her sister wouldn't have a home to come back to. If she ever did come back. Every once in a while, usually at this time of year, someone from town would make some comment about seeing her sister in the area. After two years of getting her hopes up, Nora no longer imagined Maya would show up at her door. And yet, she couldn't bring herself to move on, either.

Henry tilted his head, studying her, but he seemed to realize she didn't want to talk anymore. "Fine. Let's go."

"You don't have—"

"Going with you will give me the chance to investigate more. Dexter would know all your normal stopping points, right? It'll be due diligence." He nodded at the pepper spray. "And while it's still a mystery how the gunman used Dexter's own gun on him, we can't discount that the intruder had a gun. Spray is no match for bullets." He patted his holster.

A cold shiver ran down Nora's spine. She had tried her best to forget the masked man as she'd tossed and turned all night. All her arguments seemed to dissipate, though it seemed cruel and unusual punishment to spend an entire day with a man she'd thought would become her family. Especially since she was so desperate for a comforting hug and remembered all too well how Henry's strong arms used to warm her in an embrace.

She grabbed the two-seater kayak. This way, she wouldn't need to look into his face the entire time. She gestured for him to grab his own oar. Within ten minutes, they hit the water at a fast clip.

"You're not still planning on Sandy Cape for a stopping point, are you?" Henry asked. "Until it's officially not a crime scene—"

"No. I'll have to see if we can ride the currents fast enough to choose a different lunching spot for our guests. If we skip all the leisurely floats and games until after lunch, I think we might be able to make it work."

"That's a lot of whitewater before lunch."

She might've imagined it, but he sounded slightly concerned. "It'll also mean extra training for my guides this weekend. I think I can manage most of the rapids without your help in the kayak."

"I remember enough. I'll be fine, Nora."

The defensiveness in his voice triggered memories of too many arguments. For some reason Henry always assumed she was trying to control or critique him even if she was trying to be thoughtful. It was just enough to steel her resolve. No more lingering thoughts on his great hugs. Or his kisses. She'd never been so grateful to see the upcoming rapids so her rebellious mind would quiet down. "Right oar. Hard."

The water kicked up and they tipped precariously but didn't flip as she deftly kept them from hitting the swirling hydraulic. Her honed instinct found the fastest routes and they made record time, past Sandy Cape, past the emergency take-out. They coasted as they entered the deep canyon. The high rock walls provided a peaceful tunnel of silence, with only the occasional slap of an oar against the water. An eagle soared above their heads.

"You're still excellent at this," Henry said softly.

She ignored the sudden warmth in her cheeks. "Is it easier to be in the water now?"

"I wouldn't go that far. My leg has made some phantom pain complaints, but I'm doing all right. Don't worry about me."

He might as well have told her not to go getting attached to him. "I wasn't worried," she said. "Just curious." The wall to the left made a jagged stairlike descent into a hilly wooded area that used to be a stopping point.

"Wow," Henry said, blowing out a breath.

A mudslide had brought down several boulders about nine years ago. The massive rocks had made the area closest to land a treacherous, swirling set of new rapids. Maybe mercifully, so the locals didn't need to be reminded of tragedy. Because that spot had been where their mutual friend, Tommy Sorenson, had been murdered.

"Left. Quick strokes," she said. Like a roller coaster, they rose and fell with each wave, staying as far away from that portion of land as possible. And as fast as it began, the waters smoothed once more.

"Do you…do you think there were any similarities between Tommy and Dexter?" Henry asked. "Did Dexter seem nervous the couple of days before?"

"Besides them both being rafting guides? I don't

know. I haven't wanted to give it much thought, if I'm being honest." She knew Tommy had confided in Henry a few days before his death that he'd felt like he was being watched and asked Henry to have his back. Henry had thought he was being melodramatic but had agreed. And yet, somehow Tommy had ended up on the river alone and murdered. She knew the guilt Henry carried.

"I don't think anyone could've predicted this," she said slowly, hoping he understood she meant both Dexter's and Tommy's murders. "Do you think we're dealing with the same killer?"

"Tommy's was never staged as a suicide, so I don't think so. We can't dismiss the possibility, though. Would you mind if I interview your staff on an unofficial basis?"

"If they agree, sure. Just please don't give them any more reason to abandon ship and work for my uncle."

"Frank is trying to poach your guides?" The outrage in his voice was evident. "Totally unethical. Do you want me to talk—?"

"No." She cringed at her careless slip. When they started conversing without the same patterns of old fights, she opened up way too easily around him. They rowed in silence for a couple minutes.

"You might've noticed it is driving me a bit nuts not to be lead on this case."

His vulnerability took her off guard. "I'm sure it's hard." She exhaled as the river entered a curving portion resembling snake wiggles. "Look. We've made great time. We can stop for lunch."

"Oh. I didn't bring…"

"Don't worry. I have enough." She glanced at the bag of supplies she'd stored securely in the spot near her feet. She always brought more than enough in early spring, as she never knew when the weather might turn and delay her return.

They slid up onto the bank. The same slight erosion from the snowmelt had occurred here, but at first glance, it didn't appear she'd have much work to do to make the site ready for visitors.

Henry stepped out of the kayak and stretched. "I think I can help you tidy this place up in record time." His eyes drifted to the bag she hiked up on her shoulder. "Need to earn my keep. What's for lunch?"

She heard the eagerness in his voice. He probably hadn't so much as had breakfast. "Sandwiches. I'll get the hand-washing station set up, then you can help me move the picnic benches back before we eat." On the last river run of the season, they'd moved the tables onto higher ground before winter, partly because of erosion.

Nora disappeared between two boulders and hiked to the hiding place where they stuffed empty buckets and containers between the rocks for protection during the winter. A red bag stuffed in a crevice caught her eye. The logo matched her own. Had a rafting guide left a pack here all winter? Somebody should've reported it missing. Leaving food, sunscreen or even wipes out on the riverside went against their land use permit with the forest service.

"Everything okay?" Henry called. He appeared between the two boulders.

She reached, on her tiptoes, to grab the bag. "I think one of my guides made an overwintering mistake." Her foot began to slide on the loose rock.

Henry rushed to her side. "Please, allow me." He stretched his arm above her and tugged on the red fabric. The bag tumbled out of the crevice and fell to the ground between them. A small white cloud drifted in the air from the partially open zipper. "I don't think that's dust."

Their eyes met. Nora took a knee and examined the writing on the side of the bag closest to her. "This belonged to Dexter."

Henry grabbed a glove from a pouch on his holster belt and unzipped the red bag. Inside were several plastic packages, sealed with clear tape, of crystalline white powder. Henry leaned back and placed a hand on top of his rafting helmet.

They'd argued once before over white powder, but this looked nothing like the burn cream powder Nora had found in her sister's room all those years ago. "What do you think it is?" she finally asked.

"Meth." He blinked rapidly. "If I had to guess, we are looking at over four pounds of meth. Tens of thousands of dollars' worth." He zipped the bag up and looked over his shoulder. With one hand, he grabbed the handle of the bag, but she didn't miss the way his other hand drifted to his gun. "We might be dealing with a mobile meth ring."

"Motive for murder?"

He spun back to her, his eyes wide. "Stay close to me, Nora. I think you're in greater danger than we thought."

* * *

Henry rushed through the maze of boulders, conscious of Nora's movements behind him. He had very little chance of getting a signal with high rock walls and towering trees in the middle of nowhere, even with satellite capabilities. He tensed even more when they stepped onto the sandy beach area, out in the open. They were vulnerable here. He grabbed his phone and Dispatch answered. "Get me a direct line to the sheriff."

While he wasn't ready to admit to Nora that he had his reservations about Perry, the sheriff's office needed to be in the loop first and foremost. Nora crossed her arms over her chest and stared into the trees and foliage. Henry took five strides toward the trees and angled himself in front of her. If there was a mobile meth ring hiding in there somewhere, Dexter's murderer could be watching and waiting to take the only witness out.

Zach answered the call. "What's the situation?"

"Found a gift-wrapped package. Ten-two hundred at—" Henry, using the police code in case there was someone in the trees listening, glanced at Nora.

She frowned and looked down the river, understanding that he wanted a location to meet the deputies. "If we get back on the river, Sangster Creek will be the closest take-out point. On the Bureau of Land Management side."

"Sangster. My side. ASAP," Henry repeated.

"On it." Zach ended the call.

Henry moved to dial Perry. He hesitated, wanting to explain his intentions to Nora, yet not wanting to argue about how to do his job. Still, she had made a good point last night. Trust had to be mutual. With a little work, he felt certain they could reach a point of trust without getting too personal. Trust could be earned without feelings getting involved. He held the phone in his hand and looked into her wide eyes. "You said it yourself. We found the bag on forest service land."

Her shoulders dropped. "You need to call Perry."

"I'll admit I'm on my guard." He hoped she saw his admission as an olive branch, a trust-building step.

"I get it. Perry's in charge of the case and you have to play it safe." Her voice was slightly monotone, as if disappointed but accepting. "Thank you for keeping me in the loop. Can I hold that bag for you? I'd feel better if you had both hands free." Her eyes flicked to his holstered gun.

Her calm demeanor took him off guard. "Thanks." He handed her the bag and paced the shoreline while relaying his findings to Perry. "Can you reach this location by ATV?"

"No. That's impossible given the canyon walls before and after. I could get there by horse or on foot," Perry said, "but the space between the rocks and the trees wouldn't fit an ATV. Makes it a great hiding place when you think about it. Best way there is by boat."

"We're about to leave to head for Sangster Creek. Deputy Zach O'Brien will meet us there."

"I'm not too far away, but I don't know about meeting on Bureau land." His typical dry humor shone through. While the forest service and land management had a well-known rivalry, Perry and Henry couldn't afford to take it seriously, mostly because they'd started as friends. He wondered, though, if Perry could ever see him as an equal. They had a fifteen-year age difference and Perry still remembered Henry as a punk wannabe lawyer when they'd first met. "I can meet you at the sheriff's office."

"Sounds like a plan." Henry ended the call. There were a fair amount of wide, unmarked trails that law enforcement could use to get to the river fairly fast. It was no wonder their vehicles needed to be replaced every few years. "We better get going. Zach will be ready to pick us up soon if he takes all the dirt roads. How long to get to Sangster Creek from here?"

"Thirty minutes. Maybe longer." She held up one hand in a shrug. "I haven't been that far down the river yet with the high snowmelt." She grunted. "My scouting trip keeps getting cut short. It *should* be a very calm spot, but remember how easily new rapids form this time of year."

The river had also changed right before the ride that had shattered his leg. The boulder responsible for the surgery and subsequent months in a cast had created a set of new rapids. Each year, that particular set of rapids had grown, and was now so difficult and long that Garnet Rapids was currently off-limits. Rafters pulled out beforehand. If they wanted to continue on the Sauvage, they had to walk the mile around the rapids to get back on the river that would eventually meet up with the Salmon River and the infamous Snake River.

She hitched the red bag over one shoulder, and Henry realized her own guide bag matched the one filled with drugs. "Don't get those confused now."

He meant his words to be teasing, but she shot him a look. She opened her bag and handed him a protein bar. "Not ready for jokes yet."

His stomach growled at the offering, but his tongue wasn't exactly eager for the sawdust taste of the generic brand. She grinned at his expression. "Well, I have sandwiches, too, but I didn't think you'd be in the mood for a picnic anymore."

"Hey, I wasn't complaining." He angled his position and gestured for her to mimic him, so their backs were against the rocks as he practically inhaled the bar. He paused for a second. "Sandwiches plural? You knew I would come today?"

Her cheeks flushed. "Maybe I just wanted two sandwiches. You know how hungry I get when rafting. Besides, Bobby made them."

"The famous backpacker hoagie?" Henry eyed the bag eagerly, daring not to hope. Bobby only made those hoagies once a year as the ingredients didn't come cheap. Layer upon layer of meats, cheeses, tomatoes and expertly portioned condiments inches deep within a toasted bun. He wrapped it so tightly in clear wrap, it compressed until you were ready to unwrap and enjoy. "There is no way you could eat two of those."

"Maybe you don't know me as well as you like to think." She pursed her lips. "After last night, I thought you might try to stop me at the dock. I like to be prepared for all possibilities. I just didn't think you'd be waiting at the shed."

He feigned shock. "You were going to try to bribe an officer of the law."

Her lips twitched as if fighting a laugh. "Bribe isn't the word I would use."

With regret, he shoved the protein bar wrapper in his pocket. "Unfortunately, I don't think we can afford to take the time to eat those right now."

She tugged the opposing drawstrings and cinched her bag closed. While he kept an eye out, she secured both her bag and the matching bag of drugs inside the tandem kayak. Most of the kayaks the guides used had been fitted with a special, albeit small, storage section underneath the top of the hull. "Okay. Ready."

He lowered himself into the back seat, bracing as Garnet Rapids came to mind again. The phantom pain in his leg wasn't as bad as the real pain, he reminded himself. Besides, they would be off the river way before Garnet Rapids.

Nora moved to step into her own seat when she stopped, studying him. "How are you really, McKnight?"

Nora only used his last name when she switched into Concerned Teacher Mode, as he liked to call it. At one point, her dream had been to teach during the school year and ride the river during the breaks and summers. At least, that had been the plan when they'd first become engaged, but as far as he knew, she spent all year working for her aunt instead. He wondered why she wasn't using her degree, but now wasn't the time to ask. "Fine, Radley." He parroted back with her last name. "Ready for the Savage."

She grinned in response at his use of the river nickname. "It'll be a calm ride. You can let me do all the paddling."

"Not necessary."

"That way you can keep an eye out."

That actually wasn't a bad idea. She slipped into the seat, seamlessly grabbed her paddle, and shoved off hard enough to slide through the sand and into the water. He checked the straps of his paddle stash to make sure the oar was secure against the side of the boat. "Or I could eat a backpacker."

Her laughter bubbled up as she threw her head back, her thick braid slapping the plastic between their two seats. He couldn't help but grin at the first genuine laugh he'd heard from her in years. His heart sped up, reminding him of what was at stake. His eyes shifted to the trees around them. The echo of her laugh hovered in the air as they entered another canyon section. The slap of water against the rocks drowned it out. The waters raced faster in the narrow channel. Nora's shoulders rolled in rhythm as her paddle worked to keep them in the middle. Henry remembered the dangers of getting too close to the walls where the current could pull a rafter down underneath the water.

To the left, on forest land, the canyon wall disappeared again. She rounded a bend. At the next bank, a fisherman decked out in an oversize hat, still a good hundred feet away, held a pole. Henry frowned. "I didn't think there were roads on the USFS side to there."

"There's not, but maybe they live on the ranch nearby. We're close to the Sangster Creek pullout on the right."

His eyes narrowed at the fisherman. "This isn't

prime fishing time. Salmon aren't here yet, and he's not an angler."

"Steelhead, maybe? Want me to ask him about his fishing license?"

His gut twisted—maybe paranoia from traveling with evidence. But something didn't sit right. "No, I don't—"

The fisherman dropped his pole and turned, pulling a rifle from his side. "Nora, get down!" The bullets hit the water mere feet from the bow of the kayak. Nowhere to hide. They were on the river without any cover, too easy a target. He struggled to duck and pull his weapon while sitting at an awkward angle in the cramped seat. A bullet hit the bow. Too close.

Henry succeeded at releasing his gun and lifted his arm to take aim. Nora twisted, taking her paddle with her. She placed her paddle to the right side of the boat as the gunman fired again, this time grazing the bow. "Tandem roll," she yelled as she sucked in a breath and drove her head and body toward the water.

The side of his face hit the water and he dragged in a sharp breath a heartbeat before her momentum pulled him underneath the frigid surface. A tandem roll usually required both people to maneuver their paddles with enough force to flip back upright, but his paddle was still secured to the side of the boat. He clamped his mouth shut as the kayak floated upside down with no indication he'd get another breath any time soon.

SEVEN

Nora felt the rush of the current hard against her face but forced her eyes open. She could see maybe a few feet ahead, but that was all. The outside of her legs braced against the hull, and she fought the instinct to flip back up. The only way to hide from the gunman was to stay under water, but she didn't know how fast the current was moving them, and she probably couldn't hold her breath for much longer. Hopefully, it was true that men had ten percent more lung volume. She scanned their surroundings as best as possible, searching, hunting for boulders to avoid.

A dark shape at two o'clock. Long, thin… A tree branch underwater! She closed her eyes so her mind wouldn't play games and confuse her sense of direction. She rotated her paddle instinctively to twist in that direction. Her lungs burned. If she didn't flip them now, it would be too late. She turned her head and utilized the downward pressure with the front blade. Her knee pressed against the boat, and she snapped her hips in the same direction. The boat responded, rolling, but not with the speed she normally had with a single kayak. They weren't going to make it to the surface.

She snapped her hips again and rotated the blade for extra momentum. Her face broke the water and she inhaled greedily.

Henry gasped behind her. Nora twisted the paddle and maneuvered the kayak farther around the branch. Water rushed over top of the bow, but the log held them upright, the other branches providing only a measly bit of protection. A bullet pierced the air and Nora hunched over, bracing, until she realized the bullet had come from Henry's gun. She twisted to see they had passed the fisherman. The man was running away from the bank, likely taking cover from Henry's shot.

"Can you get us off this bundle of branches?" Henry asked, panting.

"Yes." She focused on the work of twisting and grabbing the next current that shoved them up and over the log. She ramped onto a thin bank. There was a portion of wooded area in front of the northern canyon wall. The spot had barely any room to stand unencumbered, certainly not big enough for a group of rafters, which is why it could never be a take-out spot for the company. But it would work for one boat in need of an emergency stop.

The next couple of minutes, her entire body shivered and shook, not from the cold but the adrenaline. She knew Henry was keeping an eye out for danger, yet she couldn't stop looking to either side of the river, too. He shivered alongside her, especially since he wasn't wearing a wet suit like she was. He kept his eyes on their surroundings even while he addressed her. "I think he's gone. Are you okay?"

"All things considered, yes. You?"

"That tandem roll…"

"You told me to duck. That was the only way I could think of to take cover." Her insides vibrated with more intensity as she reflected on all the many things that could've gone wrong. But at least they hadn't been shot and they hadn't drowned. "Did you see him? The gunman?"

Henry paled. "When we flipped back up, I got a closer look. He had on a camouflage face m—"

"It's him, then, isn't it? That's the same thing the murderer wore."

"I remember you said that."

She clenched her jaw in response to his nonchalance. Why couldn't he just admit that the gunman had to be Dexter's murderer? "What if he also killed Tommy?" She turned and pulled out the two red guide bags from the secured portion of the hull. They dripped with water. She opened both to check the contents. One of the drug packages seemed to have allowed a little water to leak inside but the others were sealed tight enough that they were untouched. "Did Tommy ever hint at doing drugs or selling drugs?"

Henry's frown deepened. "I…I don't—" He pulled in a breath and took out his satellite radio. "I'm going to call Zach and let him know we got held up." He turned around in a circle. "There's no way he could pick us up from here that I know of. Is there?"

"No. But we're not too far from Sangster Creek now. If you think it's safe to get back on the river…"

He continued his slow spin, scanning the trees and canyon walls, until his eyes finally met hers. "Nora, I want you to take cover while I make some calls. I need people out searching the opposite side of the bank for the gunman. If we're dealing with a mobile meth ring, there might be more gunmen out there. Once I know it's safe, we'll get back on the river." He held up the satellite phone. "Can you find a place to hide?"

"Yes." She hiked the bags over her shoulder. It felt a little childish finding a place to hide, but she recognized the wisdom in the event the gunman returned. She stepped into the foliage, careful to watch for the various plants in the region that could cause rashes and itching. Normally, they had permits that allowed rafting guides to weed those types of plants at their stopping points, but this place was designated to remain wild.

She walked right up to the canyon wall and turned around so she could keep an eye on all her surroundings. There was maybe a hundred feet of land, jam-packed with foliage and trees of all sorts, before a dead end at the rock wall. Henry's voice carried through the wind, but the filtering effects of the leaves kept her from hearing everything. He was likely talking to Zach or Perry. Her shoulders tensed.

Wasn't the gunman's rifle the same type of rifle that Perry secured to his ATV? And Zach had been adamant about insisting Dexter's death was a suicide instead of a murder. How could Henry trust either of them?

She pulled the guide bags off her shoulder. Dexter's

name, written in black marker, demanded her attention. Henry had wanted her to hide because he was worried about more drug runners out there. If they caught her and Henry, the gunmen would have no reason to keep them alive…unless she told them she knew where the drugs were. Hiding the drugs hadn't worked for Dexter, but he had been demanding more money.

Nora searched the area. A few boulders the size of garden sheds and evergreen trees that reached past the cliff side begged to be considered, but one of the dead logs caught her eye. To the right was a six-foot-tall shrub, a manzanita, if she wasn't mistaken, its pink buds hanging down in the same manner as the bleeding heart flowers. The shrub would make a perfect memory marker to help her find the log again if she needed to. The other end of the log was lodged between two boulders.

She looked in all directions, careful to make sure that no one could see her actions as she stepped between the boulders and the rock wall. She bent and stuffed Dexter's bag inside the end of the log. A rock the size of a football worked perfectly to block the opening. Too bad her phone didn't have a signal so she could properly mark the GPS location, almost like a cache to find later.

Shuffling leaves caught her ear. She popped upright and slid out from behind the rock, with only one guide bag on her shoulder now.

"Nora?" Henry called. His eyes landed on her. "Oh, good. Perry was nearby. He's on the opposite side of the river and, at least for the next mile, thinks we're safe to get to Sangster Creek. He's got someone watching from the bank as we move on."

Or, she wondered, was it a trick to make sure they came out into the open so he could shoot them?

"I think we can trust him," Henry said softly, as if he understood her facial expression. He patted his holster. "I'm still on guard. And I have good news." He grinned. "The gunman left so quickly, he left behind casings. They would've likely been washed away if Perry hadn't gotten there so quickly. He's rushing them to the lab."

Nora exhaled. Maybe Perry really wasn't a bad guy, after all. Her eyes drifted back to the boulders, the log and the manzanita shrub. Deputy Zach O'Brien would still be waiting for them at the take-out point, though. For now, she'd leave the drugs hidden. Just in case.

"Ready?" Henry held out his hand.

Without thinking, she accepted his hand to step over the rocks. Their eyes met and her mouth went dry. "It's been a long day."

He didn't let go, but only stared into her eyes, and she faltered. Maybe she should tell him that she'd hid the drugs, that she thought it would be a good test to see Zach's reaction and to keep the evidence safe for now.

"Let's get you home." He released her hand almost as if in slow motion, and Nora couldn't help but remember the last time he'd held her hand and let go like that. It had been the night they'd said goodbye to each other after breaking off the engagement. Her heart squeezed with fresh sorrow all over again.

She pressed her lips together and strode past him. "Yes. Home." Though she'd never felt so lost in her life.

* * *

Something had changed. Perhaps Nora was more frightened than she let on, but Henry had the same uncomfortable sensation he'd had in the days leading up to their breakup. She was keeping something from him. Again.

He stared after her as she strode ahead and prepped the kayak. Nora always had to take care of others, make everyone happy, as if it were her sole responsibility. Admittedly, when they were first dating, he'd loved that about her, but it had taken a whole lot of time to really get to know her and what she wanted. The same walls that he'd torn down seemed higher and thicker than ever, and yet something was off. He felt certain.

He joined her in the kayak and grabbed the paddle.

"It should be smooth sailing, as long as no one shoots…" Her voice caught. She cleared her throat and her paddle sliced through the water at a faster speed until the current caught.

"Thanks, but I'd like to keep the paddle handy in the event we need to flip over again."

"I'm sorry about that," she said. "I know your leg—"

"If I'm being honest, I've had some phantom pains, but I'm fine. Nothing you did." His heart sped up from the admission. She'd told him the truth the night before, hadn't she? The only way she would trust him is if he trusted her.

Facing forward, the trees providing privacy from the world, it seemed easier for him to share. "The water's usually not a problem. Most of my job is by land. The forest service handles the rafting and river permits and, as you also know, the river patrol—when we have someone—handles the fishing permits and river data collecting, so I think this is the first time in years I've been on the river. Maybe that's not the best thing. Face my fears and all that."

"Well, I think you've done brilliantly."

He smiled at her answer. While subtle, her verbiage sometimes shifted ever so slightly to British phrasing. She loved words like *dodgy*, *brilliantly* and *rubbish*. She'd probably watched every British drama that had been made. He'd painstakingly done his best to scrimp and save for three years, hoping to surprise her with a trip to England for their honeymoon. His chest tightened at the memory. The savings still sat, for the last three years since the split, untouched. When they'd first broken up, the temptation to use it on the best motorcycle money could afford almost won, but it hadn't seemed practical, and the last thing he'd wanted after long days in the truck was a long drive, even if on an amazing motorcycle.

"If you don't mind me asking, do you still consider teaching during the school year and being a river guide during summers?" He watched her spine straighten.

"Um, that had been the plan. But Aunt Linda needed me."

He studied the water rushing past them. "I didn't think she got divorced until recently."

She shrugged. "I want her to be happy. I have plenty of time to get to teaching."

He thought it actually became significantly more difficult to be hired the longer a person waited after getting a teaching degree, but he stayed silent.

Her sigh was so soft, he almost missed it. "I do miss spending every day on the river. Not with gunmen or discoveries of drugs, but…you know."

"I'm sorry we haven't been able to finish prepping all the sites."

"At least I got farther down the river to know what to expect. It's too bad we can't go to the regular take-out to check that off my list. It was only one more past Sangster, but we would've had to go through another set of big rapids." She exhaled. "How will the drugs we discovered help with the investigation?"

"The cache provides motive for why someone would want to kill Dexter. Beyond that…well, I'm not sure." The canyon wall on the right disappeared. A light reflected off something metallic in the distance. "I think Zach is waiting for us."

"About that. Do you trust him?"

He pursed his lips. Something about the way she asked gave him pause. "We've been over this, Nora."

"Well, I'm just wondering. If you can trust him and Perry, even though they've given you reason not to, then what does that say about me? After years of giving you nothing but reason to trust me…" She pulled in a sharp breath and the paddle slapped hard against the water. "Sorry. I didn't mean to get into our past. I really didn't." She pulled the oar up onto the bow in front of her, so their speed slowed. "The point is I should probably tell you something before we pull up on the bank and see Zach."

"Okay." The wind gusted and chilled his already wet head, causing him to shiver. But the discomfort served as a reminder. Nora had likely saved both their lives. Despite the foreboding, he forced himself to remain calm. "What is it?"

"I hid the bag of drugs."

"You did what?" His words came out almost as a shout, his peaceful intentions carried off with the breeze. Her braid flipped back. He only vaguely registered that his exclamation had likely startled her. "You hid evidence of a murder? That's obstruction of justice, Nora."

She twisted her torso so she could mostly look him in the eyes. "So, you going to arrest me? Again?" Her eyebrows raised in a challenge. She spun back around to face forward.

Despite the cold, it was as if his stomach suddenly held nothing but a plateful of habañero peppers and hot sauce. "For the last time, I didn't ever arrest you. I took you in for questioning. I couldn't be trusted to make a judgment."

Her shoulders rose almost to her ears. "You might as well finally admit that I couldn't be trusted."

"Not a good time to make a point when you just hid evidence."

"Someone wanted to kill us, probably me more than you. So, I hid the one thing that might be used as a bargaining tool to get away alive. Plus, I don't trust Zach, and I wanted to see his reaction."

Henry's shoulders sagged as she picked up the oar and made her way to the approaching bank. He replayed the words in his head. From her point of view, her reasoning probably made perfect sense. Her father had walked out never to be seen again when she was only five. She'd grown up taking care of Maya while her mother had worked two, sometimes three, jobs. Even now, after her comment about her aunt, she seemed to think everything of importance was up to her to make happen and that no one wanted to help her when *she* had a need.

And he'd failed her. Again. He'd been the one to ask her, even after she'd witnessed a murder, to guide the boat. Every question she'd had, he'd taken as a commentary on his worthiness, on his capability to do the job. He took a deep breath, purposefully compartmentalizing the feelings for another day or never. "I understand your reasoning. But, Nora, even if Zach freaks out, a reaction isn't proof of anything."

"If he pulls a gun on us, we'll know! Perry and Zach were the only ones who knew we found the drugs because you called them. Right? They knew where we were on the river. If one of them didn't shoot at us, then maybe they gave the order to someone else."

He pressed his oar into the rocky, shallow water near the bank and helped leverage them onto dry ground. He hopped out before Nora could. "Allow me." He pulled them farther up the bank and took a knee, so he could look right into Nora's face.

Bobby had been right last night, even though Henry hadn't been ready to admit it. He still owed Nora a real apology before they could ever move on. As colleagues. Friends would be too much to hope for given their past.

But if he was going to keep her safe and solve the case, they needed to reach the point of trusting each other.

"I don't want to argue with you, but I don't think Zach is going to pull a gun on us. It's probably not going to make any difference, but before we go up there I also need to tell you something." He took a deep breath. Her wet bangs had started to dry, curling and framing her eyes, wide and searching his face. The past was in the past. This was simply sharing an analysis, but the words still caught in his throat. Why did he feel like he was about to put his heart in mortal danger?

EIGHT

Nora couldn't wait to get out of the kayak, but she felt like a heavy weight had been placed on her chest, holding her back from moving as she waited for Henry to speak. She opened her mouth to press him but stopped. If this was the old Henry, the one she'd thought she was going to marry, then that look would've meant he was struggling to be vulnerable. Something shifted, though, in him ever since he had returned to the area as a law enforcement ranger.

Henry shook his head. "Like I said, it's probably not going to make any difference."

"Would it be okay if you let me decide that? What do you need to tell me?"

His eyebrows shot up and relaxed forcefully. "Well, the night I walked in on you holding…"

She wanted to interject by saying, *A perfectly innocent substance*, but bit her lip instead.

"What you didn't know was the kind of day I had. I didn't think it mattered back then, but I had just come back from my parents'. I was wanting my mother's help in booking a…a trip."

Nora's cheeks heated as she observed Henry's discomfort. A trip? Had he been about to book their honeymoon the night their relationship fell apart? She spotted the driver's door of the deputy's vehicle swing open on the rocky ridge above them. "Henry, I think Zach is starting to wonder if something's wrong."

He pressed a hand on his forehead. "The point is that my conversation with my parents didn't go well. I thought they'd finally accepted my new career, but my dad launched into how much I'd disappointed him by not going to law school like *the plan*." He blew out a breath. "And I'd had some feedback that day from my boss that wasn't all good. So, when I showed up that night, I had certain expectations about what our interaction would be like and instead—"

"I think I can fill in the gaps." Nora's mouth fell open, imagining his state of mind that night. "You were trying to prove yourself."

"I didn't think that at the time, Nora. I convinced myself I was doing the right thing, by the book. And, if I'm being a hundred percent honest, I was hurt you hadn't talked to me about your sister beforehand. I could see for myself Maya had been changing. In subtle ways at first, but…" He shook his head. "I thought we had laid the past to rest, but I realized I still owed you an apology for how I acted that night. And if we are going to work together like this then we need to properly put things to rest." He stood and waved at Zach to indicate all was well. Zach seemed to understand the message to stay put. Henry reached out a hand and Nora accepted.

She stood and stepped out of the kayak until they were a mere breath apart.

"You're wrong," Nora said. Her breathing grew shallow. "It does make a difference. I appreciate you telling me." The breeze irritated her eyes and she blinked away the moisture threatening to appear. Allergies, probably. She hesitated, not sure she wanted to continue the conversation, but he'd put everything on the table, so she felt compelled to do the same. "You probably won't believe me, but I didn't see the way my sister was changing. Not really. When I had the feeling that something was off, I didn't want to bring it to you. I knew you had enough on your plate."

"You've never liked asking for my help."

She stared at the ground and pulled her hand out of his. "We'd both stopped talking by then anyway. Grown apart. It wasn't anyone's fault." She felt like she was back at the lodge parking lot, watching the line in his chin deepen as he looked away and told her the best course would be breaking up. This conversation was too similar for comfort. "Consider the matter laid to rest. We can put the personal history aside, work together and move on."

That same hard frown returned. "I'm glad you didn't let the matter go. I think I needed an excuse to bring up the things unsaid." Henry cleared his throat. "For closure, too."

"We really didn't have each other's backs when you think about it. Guess it's good we broke up." She offered a half-hearted laugh. "Zach is probably getting impatient."

Henry seemed frozen, almost statue-like, as if fighting with himself how to respond. "He can wait. I want to make sure you hear me. I'm not talking about the past just for the sake of it. We need to trust each other now. Communicate. That's the only way I'm going to keep you safe."

The gunman seemed to grow in size in her memory, a towering monster ready to kill her and everything she held dear. Her bravado faltered. She was suddenly desperate to get back to her room and lock the door and never come out. "I understand. You're right."

He glanced over his shoulder. "You remember exactly where you put the drugs, right? Was it back at the last stop?"

She nodded. "I can retrieve it."

"I'm going to need you to take me there tomorrow morning. We can bring backup," he added quickly. "For both accountability and safety." He sighed. "And I'll make every effort to help you prepare the rest of the sites, but, Nora, I'm not sure you're going to be able to start the rafting season on time. If we can't find the gunman, if this leads to something bigger…"

He was trying to prepare her for the worst. The rafting business going under was now a real possibility. She refused to fall apart in front of him. "I won't let the magazine reporter get on her flight if I can't take her on the river, but otherwise, I prepare for the best case scenario." She took a slow breath in to calm her pounding heart. "Do you really think the drugs will help find Dexter's killer? Or will his death be written off as a drug-related death? Forgotten like Tommy's?"

His face fell. "I'll never forget Tommy's death. You know that." He cleared his throat and looked away. "We can hope that a recent arrest for one of the mobile meth labs might connect the drugs to the murderer." His voice and gaze hardened. "It's a long shot, but we still need to go by the book on this."

"Hey!" Zach hollered from above. "Perry's been trying to get hold of you. He says you'll want to hear what he has to say."

Henry looked down at his satellite phone. "I got nothing."

"We're probably too close to the canyon walls for a signal," Nora said. "He's at a better vantage point." She did her best to pick up the kayak, but her arms were spent from the last hour of hard paddling. Henry grabbed the other end of the boat without her prompting, taking more than his share of the weight as they transported the gear up the hill. The moment they set the kayak on top of the SUV, Henry's phone buzzed. "Perry texted. Zach was right. He wants me to call immediately."

The rangers were used to bad phone signals and had the habit of projecting their voices loud enough for a town hall when they were communicating. Perry's greeting through Henry's phone was loud enough for Nora to hear while she strapped the kayak to the SUV. Zach stepped out of the vehicle again and tried to help her, though he didn't seem accustomed to securing a boat and kept waiting for her to give instructions.

She avoided looking Zach in the eye. She still took it personally that he disregarded her witness statement.

"I had a gut feeling that something about those bullet casings looked familiar." Perry's voice continued to carry from the speaker of Henry's phone. "I checked the crime reports. The striations looked similar to the photos I took of other casings. At another crime."

Henry scratched his head. "But nothing official?"

"No. I have a friend at the ATF office in Boise. They have the National Integrated Ballistic Information Network at their fingertips."

"You and I both know it'll take weeks to—"

"Takes them fifteen minutes to run the test, Henry. As long as it's top of the pile, and since the gunman took a shot at a law enforcement officer, we have your life at risk to thank for a priority rising to the top of the stack. I had the forensics equipment in the office to send them what they needed. They'll have results back to us in the hour."

"That's… Wow. That's great."

Zach had stopped helping and was staring at Henry, clearly engrossed in the conversation, as well. Nora tried to move past him to finish tightening the tie-downs, but it was as if she had become invisible to the deputy. Her damp braid clung to the back of her neck and she accidentally hit him with it as she swung it around her shoulder. "Sorry."

He grumbled but stepped out of her way.

"I know you don't work in forensics. Do you know what that means?" Perry's voice came through the static.

Henry rolled his eyes for dramatic effect and Zach laughed, clearly having overheard. "The hammer or firing pin of each rifle has a unique striking pattern," Henry responded. "I'm fully educated, Perry."

"I guess you were going to be a lawyer. They probably go nuts over stuff like that."

Henry unclipped his helmet and scratched his head. He turned to face Nora while he spoke into the phone. "While you wait on your results, I'd like to assemble a team tomorrow. We weren't able to bring the drugs we found back to land—after the shooting and all. The drugs are in a safe place, but I think we need more hands to make sure we don't get fired on when we retrieve them."

"We definitely need a team, Henry, but we're going to do more than retrieve the drugs." Perry sighed. "My ATF contact just dinged me with an email. It's only preliminary and needs to be confirmed, but the bullets that were used to shoot at you today *did* match a former crime."

"You don't sound very happy about that." Henry approached the SUV and gestured with his thumb that they should probably get going. Zach nodded and got into the driver's seat while Henry opened the backseat and gestured for Nora to get inside. "What's the lead? Who shot at us?"

"The striations on the shell casings match the firing marks on the bullets used to kill Tommy Sorenson."

Nora gasped and spun to Henry. His face drained of all color.

"Whoever wants you two dead also killed your rafting friend, Tommy," Perry said.

* * *

Henry tightened his holster and checked his ammunition. The morning air seemed to suspend the moisture from last night's intense rain. The cold and humidity were no match for the layers he wore today. This time, he was going to be prepared if he needed to *dunk* for cover. He hustled to the employee lodge office where the front door was propped open.

A low male voice spoke urgently. "I think we both know this place is hanging by a thread. It's time to call—"

"I've already told you I can't let Aunt Linda down. She's counting on me." Nora's voice was easily recognizable.

"Please remember you're not the only one in the world that cares about her."

Henry knocked on the doorframe and stepped into the office where Bobby and Nora faced off from opposite sides of the office countertop. A raft made out of paperclips caught his attention. Since he'd last visited, a new set of people had been added, made out of brads and clips, with mechanical pencils as their spines. "Nice decorations."

Nora's cheeks flushed. She'd frequently told him she found it impossible to stay still, and her creativity spilled over into unusual areas, like office supplies, during any downtime. Once again, he wondered why she wasn't teaching elementary in the schools yet. Maybe it had something to do with what Bobby had been trying to tell her, but his urgency had sounded odd to Henry. Bobby knew the upcoming visit from the travel reporter would mean a lot of publicity, but was the rafting company in such dire straits? Or was Bobby trying to make a play for the company—and maybe Nora's aunt—while they were in a vulnerable position?

Bobby shifted uncomfortably under Henry's gaze but gave a nod as a way of greeting. Henry's father may have pushed him too hard to follow his legacy as a lawyer, but he'd learned a lot from his dad. At the moment, the lesson of keeping enemies close came to mind. Suspected enemies, in this case. He was using the same philosophy today for the team trip on the river.

Nora wouldn't understand. Perry had opened the cold case wide, so Henry didn't find the man's behavior nearly as suspicious. Zach, though, needed to be on today's trip. If he slipped up, Henry would be watching.

"Hey, Bobby," Henry said, "did Nora tell you we are taking a team out on the river?"

"Yes. I don't understand what's taking so long to wrap up the scene and let us out there, but sure. Whatever it takes to get on the water."

Nora and Henry shared a look. So she hadn't shared with Bobby that Dexter and Tommy's murder were connected in some way. That was actually to their benefit. Perry said he would wait twenty-four more hours to see if they could turn up any other leads before he needed to call in the FBI for assistance. Once the FBI was involved, Henry would be officially off the case. Today was Henry's last chance to help.

"We could use another rafting guide," Henry said on the fly. "Another guide would mean that we could spread out more as a team, cover more ground."

Nora's eyes widened. "Who all is coming?"

"Can you do without Bobby here for a day?" He tried to communicate with his eyes that it wasn't a good time to ask who was coming. By the way Nora's eyebrows jumped, he was a little worried how she would interpret his expressions.

"Are you feeling okay?" she asked. "You look like you're going to be sick. Do you need breakfast?"

Henry released a breath. He'd never been good at subtlety and subtext. He produced a brown bag. "Actually, no. I brought you breakfast from town." He set the bag on the countertop. She pulled out the enclosed scone and to-go thermos of tea with a gasp.

"Tea and a cinnamon scone? Thank you." Her eyes flickered to his, and a soft smile formed. So, she still thought of tea and scones as the ultimate comfort then. For some reason, the knowledge that some things hadn't changed was reassuring. Nora broke off a chunk of the scone and offered Bobby a portion, which he declined. "If you're willing to be a guide," she said, "it's up to you. We were talking about giving the trainees the day off anyway. What's left of them, that is." She turned and offered Henry a portion of the scone, as well.

"No, it's for you. What do you mean 'what's left of them'?"

Bobby's shoulders drooped. "We've just found ourselves short-staffed for raft season now." Bobby and Nora exchanged a look that held its own secret code.

Henry's chest tightened. There was camaraderie between the two of them. Nora needed help with something, that much was obvious, but Henry was no longer her confidant. Asking others for help had always been her last resort anyway. So, whenever she *had* asked him for help, she'd done it so rarely, he'd have done anything he could to answer her requests. And if he couldn't help, he'd encouraged her to ask someone who could. Was that all Bobby was doing? Taking the place that was once his and encouraging her to ask for help?

"I guess we're both yours for the day," Nora said.

Despite the exhaustion from yesterday, he'd tossed and turned all night remembering the closeness and the way Nora had stared into his eyes. He could see she'd truly forgiven him. It was like a heavy weight he hadn't known existed had finally been released. Then, when she'd transitioned into saying she was ready to move on, that weight had unexpectedly shifted and punched him in the gut.

As much as he wanted to deny it, some part of him had always imagined that if they'd ever worked past their hurts, he'd feel free. His heart hadn't let him sleep until he'd admitted to himself it was a lie.

Bobby walked past Henry and slapped him on the shoulder, jarring him out of his thoughts. "I'll go grab my gear. A little time out on the water is just the medicine I need. Always." He sauntered out of the office, whistling.

Nora popped the last bite of scone in her mouth and took a sip of tea. "Thank you for this, but we should get going. Bobby will only take a minute to get ready. We're wasting daylight." She walked around the counter, her red guide bag over her shoulder. "Why do you need another guide?"

"I thought it would be best to go in groups of two. I meant what I said about wanting to cover more ground. More eyes on this means more chances we'll find something. We have one day, Nora. We need to stop at as many sites as possible and hope we find another lead for the town's sake. You know what happens once this hits the news tonight. If we don't have it solved…"

"Tourism will take a huge hit." She bit her lip. "The whole town might as well file for unemployment at that point."

"It won't be pretty." He accompanied her outside as she locked the office door. The sound of an engine approaching caught her attention, and she looked over her shoulder and stiffened. "Bringing Perry along, I understand. Deputy Carl Alexander knows his way around the river. But Zach?" Her eyes narrowed. "Is this a 'keep your enemies close' thing?"

Henry straightened but kept his surprise muted. Maybe she understood him better than he'd realized. Bobby approached with a two-person kayak lifted high over his head, fully decked out with tie-dyed swim shorts and a shirt with a funny image of a river otter in rafting gear. The man had been known to wear wigs and tutus, if necessary, to get children smiling on a rafting trip. But today wasn't about having a good time.

Henry's legs took on a will of their own, slowing the pace to the dock. Even with the warm clothing, he didn't want to ever have to flip in a kayak again. Having no control and wondering if another boulder was going to appear at any moment, this time to shatter his skull instead of his leg, replayed in his mind too often.

"I chose a raft for us this time," Nora said softly. "I figured we'd have an easier time taking cover if necessary. That flip under water…"

"It's forgotten." Henry exhaled, not realizing until now that he'd been holding his breath, but the idea of a raft instead of a kayak eased his mind slightly. As long as he didn't have to straddle the outside edge with his leg exposed. "Let's just pray we find what we need today, for everyone's sake, and stay safe while we do it."

NINE

Nora tried to act as carefree as Bobby but found it impossible. She knew too much.

Carl waved at Bobby, clearly having picked his rafting partner, and pointed to the back seat of a kayak. Zach O'Brien stood with Perry next to a two-person raft. The two men she trusted the least standing side by side brought her an odd sense of comfort. If Henry wanted to keep potential enemies close, then having them in one boat made it easier to keep an eye on them.

Henry put his fists on his hips, ready to give out orders. He was like a force of nature, prepared to confront challenges head-on and expecting everyone to attack life with the same level of passion. She both admired and feared the tendency. Sometimes he pushed too hard, not realizing his plans weren't always best.

She surveyed the river. The currents had shifted ever so slightly, an indication of changes to watch. Somewhere along the river, the overnight rain had loosened muddy banks. Bobby knew what to watch out for, and Carl seemed to have experienced enough with kayaks to be a good partner in the rougher waters. Perry was her only concern, but he'd been the one to warn her about the change to the whitewater near Garnet Rapids.

Her neck prickled with unbearable tension. How many days had she been trying to get one uninterrupted trip all the way to Garnet to see what they were dealing with? Yet another reminder of what was at stake if Henry didn't solve the murders today. If she had to tell her aunt to come home, that would be like admitting failure, something Bobby didn't seem to understand. Aunt Linda would be coming home to see the business she'd started close its doors. Nora would never share a home with Maya again.

"So, we've already paired off," Henry said. "We've got an officer able to cover each guide. We don't expect any problems today with such a show of force."

Nora's chest fluttered. If they didn't expect force, then why did each guide need cover? She pointed at Perry. "He's not a guide."

"I've kept my certifications up." Perry crossed his arms across his chest. "Zach just needs to do what I say, and he'll be fine."

Henry clapped his hands. "Okay. Nora will lead the way, but we are going to stop at every site possible with a perspective the FBI didn't have last time. Think like a guide." His eyes turned to her. "That's how we found the package yesterday. Let's see if either Tommy or Dexter left us more clues than that."

Bobby frowned hard but didn't ask questions.

She stepped closer to Bobby. "I didn't know what I was allowed to share," she said softly so only he could hear. "Now that you know that there might be danger today, you can back out. I can get a bigger boat and take Carl with us, too."

"Don't worry about me. One cop is enough, but we've got four. I like those odds against anything man can throw my way." Bobby nodded at the river. "Now the river is another matter, but you know that's why I like it."

Bobby had actually been the one to lead her to Christ when she was in her late teens. She'd come back from her first year of college a mess. He'd told her he loved riding the river's waves because, like life, control was an illusion. The whitewater reminded him that only one was in control. He could try to choose a path, but in the end, he needed to do his best, fear the Lord and enjoy the ride. Nora had never forgotten. Ironic that Bobby and Henry seemed to be challenging the very flexibility they both seemed to appreciate about her.

"Let's get going," Henry said. "Nora, take the lead."

She rushed forward and situated Henry in the middle of the raft while she took the back portion. No one needed to be right in the small front bow, at least not for now. Once they were a good fifty feet in front of the other boats, she leaned forward in the hope that the wind wouldn't take her words and carry them to the others. "I don't know what to expect from the river, but I'm going to need you to paddle today. Are you feeling ready?"

He twisted and offered a smile. "I told you. It's all coming back to me."

She leaned back and focused on the water. They didn't bother stopping at Sandy Cape since they'd al-

YOU pick your books –
WE pay for everything.
You get up to FOUR New Books and TWO Mystery Gifts...absolutely FREE

Dear Reader,

I am writing to announce the launch of a huge **FREE BOOKS GIVEAWAY**... and to let you know that YOU are entitled to choose up to FOUR fantastic books that WE pay for.

Try **Love Inspired® Romance Larger-Print** books and fall in love with inspirational romances that take you on an uplifting journey of faith, forgiveness and hope.

Try **Love Inspired® Suspense Larger-Print** books where courage and optimism unite in stories of faith and love in the face of danger.

Or TRY BOTH!

In return, we ask just one favor: Would you please participate in our brief Reader Survey? We'd love to hear from you.

This FREE BOOKS GIVEAWAY means that we pay for *everything!* We'll even cover the shipping, and no purchase is necessary, now or later. So please return your survey today. You'll get **Two Free Books** and **Two Mystery Gifts** from each series to try, altogether worth over **$20!**

Sincerely

Pam Powers

Pam Powers
For Harlequin Reader Service

Complete the survey below and return it today to receive up to **4 FREE BOOKS** and **FREE GIFTS** guaranteed!

▼ DETACH AND MAIL CARD TODAY! ▼

FREE BOOKS GIVEAWAY
Reader Survey

1

Do you prefer books which reflect Christian values?

◯ YES ◯ NO

2

Do you share your favorite books with friends?

◯ YES ◯ NO

3

Do you often choose to read instead of watching TV?

◯ YES ◯ NO

YES! Please send me my Free Rewards, consisting of **2 Free Books from each series I select** and **Free Mystery Gifts**. I understand that I am under no obligation to buy anything, as explained on the back of this card.

❏ **Love Inspired® Romance Larger-Print** (122/322 IDL GQ36)
❏ **Love Inspired® Suspense Larger-Print** (107/307 IDL GQ36)
❏ **Try Both** (122/322 & 107/307 IDL GQ4J)

FIRST NAME	LAST NAME

ADDRESS

APT.#	CITY

STATE/PROV.	ZIP/POSTAL CODE

EMAIL ❏ Please check this box if you would like to receive newsletters and promotional emails from Harlequin Enterprises ULC and its affiliates. You can unsubscribe anytime.

LI/LIS-520-FBG21

© 2020 HARLEQUIN ENTERPRISES ULC ® and ™ are trademarks owned and used by the trademark owner and/or its licensee. Printed in the U.S.A.

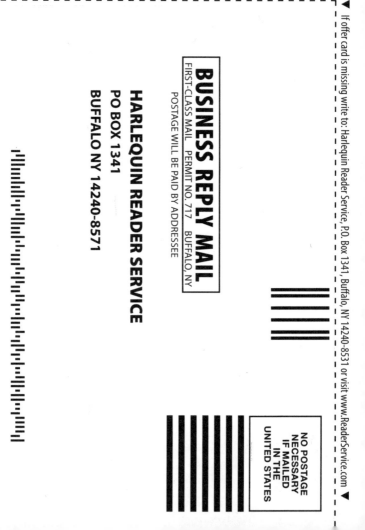

ready searched that area top to bottom. The upcoming rapids of The Killer rushed with extra ferocity but not enough to bump it up a level of classes. Henry moved quickly and without argument at each paddle command. Toward the end, a shadow she hadn't seen before hovered underneath a new, swirling hydraulic right in their path.

The raft spun sideways and she felt the shift before visually seeing the raft begin to lift on one side. They were stuck on a rock. Barely, but enough that the rapids were about to capsize them right on top, a dangerous proposition. "High side!" she called out as a command.

She kept her hand firmly around the hard end of the paddle, lest she lose control and it hit Henry. The ends of the oars were hard enough to take out a tooth or to bloody a nose if not careful. She shoved her foot against the raft to propel herself to the downstream side. They needed weight on the side of the raft where water flowed immediately. Henry seemed to have frozen, dangerously teetering and about to be swallowed by the water. "High side, Henry!"

He blinked and dove her way, the paddle underneath him. The waters grabbed the edge they'd both clambered on, swirled the raft around and spat it out on the other side of the rock. They bounced over one remaining baby rapid and the waters calmed. Henry leaned back over the rampart and closed his eyes. "That was close."

"You did great." She twisted to see that Bobby and Carl had learned from their experience and deftly taken the rougher current, the one that avoided the chance of capsizing. Zach's eager grin couldn't be missed as he hooted and hollered with every bounce. Perry seemed to be laughing along with him.

"Guess they figure they might as well enjoy the ride," Bobby hollered over the dulling roar.

Except something didn't look right. They weren't lifting up out of each wave like they should have been. "Bob—"

"I see it now." He dug his paddle in the water and shouted commands to Carl. The kayak spun around as if on a dime and they fought against the current to get closer.

"What's going on?" Henry popped up on his knees, squinting.

"Something seems wrong with Perry's boat. I don't think they were laughing but shouting. They're trying to let us know they have a problem, but it's impossible to get back into those rapids. We can't go that far upstream. The current is too strong, too fast."

"We have to try." Henry sat upright and moved to the front of the bow. "Tell me what to do."

"Left!" She didn't hesitate, fighting against the waters as they tried to catch up to Bobby. Once turned around, she could see the raft had already capsized. But how? She held her breath, paddling faster. *Please keep them safe*. The left side of Perry's raft crumpled and flipped bow-over-stern until it was spat out over a boulder. No one was in the raft, but she couldn't see the two men anywhere. The last wave of the rapids beat the raft into a piece of flat and limp plastic that was half immersed in the waters.

"What!" Henry tried to stand in their raft but fell back down. "What is happening?"

"They're not in the boat." Nora lifted her oar, losing the fight against the current. "I've never in my life seen a raft sink. There's four distinct chambers in a raft. If one of them gets punctured the others keep the—"

Henry's eyes widened. "You're saying this was on purpose." He put his hand above his eyebrows, searching the banks. "Perry!"

"There," Bobby said, allowing the current to shove his kayak back until it was side by side with Nora. He pointed with his oar. "I see them. They've made it out. Look!" On top of a rock closest to the bank, Perry stood, drenched, waving. Zach was on his hands and knees, sputtering on the rock. She pushed through the burning in her arms, attempting to paddle closer again. "He's bleeding."

Bobby leaned over the side of his kayak and caught the flimsy raft drifting past. "Worthless now." He fought to lift it and study it, rivulets of water pouring over the side of his kayak. He finally dropped the deflated raft back into the water. "This was punctured and resealed with junky glue on all four sides."

Henry sank down to sitting. "Does that mean what I think it means?"

Nora fought to process the news herself. "Someone wanted them to drown in those waters."

Henry's satellite radio squawked. He grabbed it and clicked it on in one fast motion.

"We're okay," Perry said with a huff.

"Your raft was sabotaged."

"I figured that news flash out as soon as we started to sink in the middle of The Killer. That raft is self-bailing but took on water faster than it could drain." Perry took a deep breath before continuing. "Zach has a head injury—he didn't latch his helmet on and lost it in the water—but will be fine. I've already got Dispatch sending a car to the closest ranch nearby. We'll hide and watch till help comes."

"They're okay?" Nora asked.

Henry nodded as Perry's voice filled the line. "Someone doesn't want us on the river today, McKnight. Get the package, keep an eye out, and get the drugs to evidence. You're the last chance for the town, Henry. The FBI will be notified tonight. The media will catch on within hours of that."

"Just get Zach patched up and stay safe yourself." The waters picked up speed, and Nora worked the paddle without him to turn them face-forward.

"Over and out."

"Over and out." Henry returned the radio to his holster belt. No easy feat given the life jacket in the way.

"Stick to the plan?" Nora asked. He simply nodded and Nora shouted as much to Bobby and Carl. She guided them in the waters in relative silence for the next few minutes until Henry picked up his paddle to join her.

She moved to join him in the middle of the boat. Side by side, they could only take their respective positions to paddle, not to mention the space was a bit tight. That could only mean one thing. She wanted to talk without the others overhearing. "What's up?" Henry asked.

"You were keeping Perry and Zach together because, even though you didn't want to admit it, you thought it would be easiest to keep an eye on them that way, right?"

He sighed. "Nothing gets past you, Radley." The use of her last name was something they used to joke about when she'd first interned as river patrol. He'd said that's how they would keep their work and personal lives separate. Last name at work, first name when off duty. "I wasn't so much worried about Perry anymore as I was Zach. But neither one of them would risk getting in a raft they had sabotaged themselves, especially in The Killer."

"You're forgetting that Bobby was a surprise addition. Maybe they thought they were riding with us instead and had no choice but to stick it out and hope for the best."

"By your way of thinking that makes Carl a suspect, as well."

"He has no motive, though," she said. "And he didn't seem to care where he was placed." She pointed ahead. "Remember how we used to think the site where Tommy was killed had been closed off to us as a mercy?"

"I never thought that." There had been many times if he could've easily accessed the site, he would have.

"Other guides did. We didn't want the constant memory. But you said no one looked at Tommy's case from a guide's perspective. It wouldn't be easy... I would need you to follow every single direction I call out and be ready for anything, but—"

"You think you can get us to the site of Tommy's murder?"

She nodded. "I think Bobby has the skills to, as well. I don't know about Carl, but he worked as a guide for years—for my uncle's company—but still, he seems to have kept up basic skills from what I can tell."

Unlike him. She didn't say it, but she didn't need to.

His chin jutted. "It's all coming back to me. I maneuvered the high side. It just took me an extra moment to understand what was happening. Tell me and I'll do it."

"Aye, aye, captain?" she asked with a laugh.

"Aye, aye." He gave a nod.

"It's not going to be easy, but if you do exactly as I say I think we can do it." She scooted out of the middle and resumed her post, repeating her plan to Bobby. He enthusiastically shook his paddle in the air to indicate he understood.

The rapids up ahead appeared extra foreboding compared to yesterday. Boulders seemed stacked up like blocks in front of the site Nora had referenced. Henry's throat went dry despite the humidity.

"We're going to get as close to those boulders as we can and let the current whip us around. Then we paddle like our lives depend on it."

Her reassuring tone did nothing to calm his nerves. She began shouting out commands rapidly. The strain in her voice made the hairs on his neck stand straight. He kept his eyes on the front of the raft, not allowing his focus to veer to the water or to the rocks they were rushing toward. The scone he'd eaten at the bakery while he'd waited for the cashier to bag the to-go order for Nora threatened to make a reappearance. But he could trust Nora. She knew her stuff. He could let her take the lead.

"I said left!"

Henry slid across the seat and paddled intensely on the other side, determined. She'd asked for help and he was going to prove he still had what it took. That he'd conquered the fear. His arms began to burn after only a couple minutes.

"Stop!" Nora cried out.

He pulled up the oar and felt the current roar underneath his feet. The waters swirled and the raft spun and kicked them out toward the bank. Nora dove past him, her feet barely hitting the bow as she bent and snagged the rope on the D-line. She launched herself in the air like a soaring ballerina, except with water shoes and her favorite neon-pink life jacket and helmet. Her foot barely touched the sandy bank and she crumpled, rolling on the ground.

"Nora!" He jumped to his feet, letting the paddle fall to the bottom of the raft.

Suddenly, the raft tugged toward land and Henry almost fell backward. Nora struggled to her feet, tugging on the rope with fierce determination lining her forehead. "The undertow is strong and wants to pull it back into a hydraulic. We need to hurry. Then be ready to help Bobby."

Henry ignored the vibration in his chest that told him to hunker down and wait for land. He forced his heavy legs to move and launched himself into the air, as well. He landed a mere six inches beside Nora. He stood and grabbed the rope with her and felt the massive tug-of-war the river wanted to play.

"Faster! Bobby will need the space to get in."

Except the kayak was already past the opening, fighting once again to return upstream.

"They missed the current." Nora's voice warbled.

"Meet up at the next site," Henry hollered, pulling the rope closer.

"Oh, no. Henry, look."

The D-ring on the bow of the boat seemed to have frayed the rope, and then the rope went slack. Nora fell back. Their raft, now free of the rope, began to slide out of the bay with the current. Henry kicked off his back foot. That raft was their only hope for getting out.

His hands hit the bow of the boat, but the raft moved too quickly. His lower torso slammed against the water with enough force to shove most of the air from his lungs. The water grabbed his feet and tugged with the greatest force he'd ever felt, pulling him underneath the frigid waters. His fingers dug into the handles on the side of the raft, but the boat and life jacket were no match for the deadly undertow.

He lifted his chin and pulled in the deepest breath he could muster before the waters swirled over his head, pulling him farther under. *Is this it, Lord?* He spun around in the water, blinking rapidly, trying to see past the bubbles. His heart squeezed with fear. He may not have remembered much from the summer before he'd shattered his leg, but he knew that aerated water wouldn't allow him to float back to the surface.

The river continued to draw him deeper under until a different current punched him in the chest and shot him forward, right toward two boulders. Instinct told him to put his feet out, but his legs refused, remembering the pain of impact at high speed all too well. There was a space between the boulders, maybe if he could—

The bubbling water spun him again, so he couldn't see, but something snagged him and his body stilled. Except the water continued to pound him right in the chest. Over and over. He glanced down at the rocks that had him pinned right around his waist.

TEN

Nora dropped the guide bag from her back. She pulled out the throw bag and pitched it as far as her arm allowed, hoping it would hit where she'd seen Henry go under. "Rope!" Except the bag filled with unraveling rope disappeared under the water. It was supposed to float, which meant only one thing. The undertow went deeper than she'd thought, right where he'd disappeared.

She searched the waters, letting the rope pull her along the bank. *Lord, help me understand the currents once again.* There. The red bag popped back up. The end of the rope shook in her hand. If she was right, the current would eventually spit something heavier, like Henry, out, too, right into the boulders at the far edge of the bank.

No, anything but the boulders.

She pulled the rope, gathering it as best she could as she ran along the shore. The soles of her feet felt every bump of the rough pebbles through her water shoes as she hurdled tree logs blocking her path. She hesitated before she climbed the first steep boulder, violent splashes of water kicking up at her shins. One wrong move and she would slip under the water, as well.

She grabbed her edge of the rope and tied it around her waist. If she was going down, so be it. She would be Henry's only hope. She used both hands, clawing and sliding against the edges and moss on the boulders. Once at the top, she took off her helmet and grabbed a nearby hefty rock to place inside. Her fingers shook as she clicked the strap to hold it within. The helmet wouldn't go very far under water, but it was possible, if Henry was stuck underneath...

She leaned over as much as she could manage and let the weighted helmet hang, suspended in air. Using a swinging motion, she launched the helmet like a pendulum until it dropped right into the current she'd spotted. The rope slid through her fingers, pulling the helmet below the surface. Nora dropped down to a squat and pressed her feet against the second boulder to stay steady. If the rope started tugging her under the water, she'd need to act fast to untie it from her waist. If that were even possible.

"If you're down there, keep your eyes open!"

The rope tugged with the weight of a sudden catch... or it was trapped in a current between the boulders and she was pulling against impossibilities. Nora leaned back, pressing her heels deeper into the second rock. Her legs shook from the effort. The rope slowly began to tighten around her waist. Should she give up? Should she untie the rope? She closed her eyes. *Please don't take him, too.*

A cry escaped her lips from the effort. She pulled

on the rope between her legs and looked down at the churning water. Hot pink! She could see the hot pink helmet, struggling to come up, and fingers wrapped around the rope.

"Henry!"

A hand on the line just above the splashing water appeared. The rope dug into her waist. Henry's face surfaced, pulling in a hungry breath of air. Coughs burst out of his mouth before he gasped, dragging in another breath.

"Brace your feet between the rocks!" Her voice shook with fear. They weren't out of danger yet. She still needed to get him out of the water, but he might not have much self-control if he'd inhaled water. The muscles flanked by her shoulder blades threatened to revolt, and her forearms burned like they might combust, but she forced her raw hands to keep pulling the rope upward.

The moment Henry's shoe braced against the boulder, the rope slackened ever so slightly. Nora finally lay back, her entire body shaking from the effort. The top of the boulder was rounded, having no sharp edge like the other side. She slid off the boulder to land so she could use the rock like a pulley system for the hardest portion of getting Henry fully out of danger.

The minutes felt like hours, but the moment she spotted Henry on top of the boulder, she collapsed onto her knees on the bank. She raised her face to the sky, her eyes closed. "Thank you," she whispered.

Coughs still racked Henry as he splayed prone on top of the boulder. She untied the rope from around her waist and gathered it up only to find her pink helmet bobbing on the water. The rock to weigh it down must have slipped sideways out of the harness.

Henry propped himself up on one elbow. "I've never been so thankful your power color was neon pink."

She laughed. All rafting guides liked to wear their favorite color. "What happened?" She climbed the boulder nearest to him and sat, facing downstream. She didn't want to stare at the churning waters that had almost taken his life.

"The current dragged me under and then..." He bent over and fingered his waistband.

"Your belt. Your holster is missing!"

"The belt was caught, wedged between the boulders at the closest point." Rivulets of water still streamed down his face from his helmet and drenched hair. "I finally managed to get the belt off, but I couldn't wiggle myself free. The force of the current kept my chest pinned. I grabbed your helmet when it hit my elbow." He turned to her. "I almost missed it, but I knew immediately what it was. My arms weren't caught in the current, or I'd have been done for. I pulled for all I was worth until I got free." He eyed the rope as she stuffed it back into the red throw bag. "How were you strong enough to pull me up?"

She shook her head. "The better question is what were you thinking?" She blew out an exasperated breath. "If you weren't still recovering, I'd be tempted to smack you. You could've been killed. I never would've even brought you here if I didn't think you remembered—"

"I knew we needed that raft. I didn't have time to question my instinct. I felt I had to try." He waved at the empty river ahead of them. "We're surrounded by cliffs on either side. The only way someone is going to rescue us is if they have the same skills you do, which has become obvious is pretty rare. If Bobby couldn't do it, then what chance is there?"

"Don't give me too much credit. I know these waters like the back of my hand. I keep my skills up, but since you've lost your phone…"

Henry groaned. "Don't remind me."

"And since we were obviously sabotaged—"

"Wait. What?"

She turned to face him. "Just like I've never seen a raft deflate like Perry's did, I've also never seen a rope shred like that in the D-ring. If we ever get our hands on that boat again, I'm sure we'll see someone tampered with it. Cut a slit or something in it. All the new equipment in the last decade is made with safety in mind. This wasn't an accident."

"But they couldn't have known it would happen here."

"No. But if we had capsized in the rapids—which you remember happens often—I wouldn't have been able to flip the boat back up, either. If we'd gotten trapped underneath…" She shrugged, unwilling to list all the ways they could have been injured or killed if their safety equipment wasn't up to par. "A lot can go wrong with one act of sabotage. Best-case scenario, we would've lost the boat at the next stop when I went to pull it in. We still would've been trapped."

Henry dropped his head into his hands. "Someone wants to make sure we can't retrieve the drugs for evidence."

A new thought came to mind. "Henry, I don't think we can afford to wait around for someone to retrieve us. If Perry's boat and our boat were sabotaged…"

His eyes widened. "Bobby and Carl might be in danger, too. And I can't even send them a warning." He frowned. "There doesn't seem to be much of a choice other than to wait. Do you have an idea how to get out of here?"

"There's only one way to get out of here." She grimaced. "How long do you need to recover? Because you're not going to like it."

Henry didn't want to hear her solution quite yet. He didn't want to so much as look at the water, and if he had noise-canceling headphones he would use them to block out the sound of the waves. Every muscle hurt and he couldn't stop the low-grade shiver. His body felt like a vibrating engine trying to fully start again. Movement would help, even though he wanted the cloud above to move and bake him with sunshine. He groaned. "Let's do what we came here to do so it's not a total waste."

Nora swiveled her feet around to go down the set of boulders. "I'm not sure we should get our hopes up. Someone didn't want us to retrieve the drugs, but if the two murders are connected, they didn't seem to care about this stop."

"You don't think there's anything worth finding here

since someone has been one step ahead of us this whole time."

"Basically." She carefully descended, reached the ground and turned around to offer a hand to him.

"Thank you for the thought, but if I slip, you're not catching or helping me. I'd flatten you."

She rolled her eyes. "You don't know," she teased and stepped back.

"I think I really do." He had at least fifty pounds on her. The laugh bubbled in his chest, irritating his lungs, and he had to balance precariously on the rock as he fought through a set of coughs. "Well," he said at last, "I think that helped get the last of the water out of my system."

"Laughter is the best medicine?" She fished out her water bottle from the guide bag, took off the lid and offered it to him. "You might want a drink of some clean water."

He accepted but forced himself not to guzzle the entire thing down. His own water bottle was still stowed in the raft, probably almost to the Snake River by now. She tossed him a plastic-wrapped sandwich. "Sorry. I made them this time. Not Bobby."

He didn't care. Though the amount of mustard she'd used on the roast beef sandwich should be illegal. "How can you like both bland scones and hot and spicy mustard? My sinuses are clear now."

She barked a laugh as she finished her sandwich as if it were plain toast. "That's why. Best springtime congestion cure there is, in my opinion. Let me know if you need any wasabi almonds." She wandered into the trees. The thick layer of brown leaves and rotted wood seemed to indicate they'd been the only ones to visit the area since the mudslide had produced the extra rapids.

He didn't stop to look at the spot he knew Tommy had been shot. As soon as his active law contract with the sheriff had been in effect when he'd accepted the enforcement ranger position, he'd requested Tommy's file. He'd poured over the photos so often, it felt surreal to be in the place they'd been taken.

He glanced down at his indestructible watch, glad it seemed to have lived up to promises. While he had confidence that Carl would keep Bobby safe, Nora had a point. It did seem as if someone was picking them off one by one. Hopefully, Bobby was safe since Henry had unexpectedly invited him. "Who could have had access to both your boat and Perry's ahead of time? Perry brought his own boat from his field office."

She shook her head. "I'm not sure. I had set up my boat before I went in the office to make our lunches and chat with Bobby. It probably sat out there for a good hour unattended, but I don't know about Perry's raft. It'd be pretty risky to sabotage his own boat, but if he was confident about his skills in the water…"

"He'd still have someone with him." Henry clicked the timer feature on his watch. "Let's take ten minutes then try whatever your idea is to catch up with Carl and Bobby." Even as he said it, he fought to ignore the sudden tightness in the back of his neck and shoulders. He really didn't want to get back on the water. "It's time to think like a guide. What places would a guide notice that an FBI agent wouldn't?"

Nora turned to him, an eyebrow raised. "Do you miss being a guide at all?"

He scoffed and shook his head. *The best thing about being a guide was meeting you.* He came to a sudden halt at the surprising thought.

Nora had already looked away, though. "I thought so, but was just curious." She reached up to examine some areas in the rocks.

"Watch out for black widows. This is the time of year."

She grabbed a stick and poked several locations in the rocks just above her head. Henry went in the opposite direction to all the spots in the trees that Tommy might have stashed a bag like Dexter had. His wrist vibrated with his ten-minute alarm after what seemed like mere moments. He'd made it as far as the rock face that blocked them from the rest of the world. He looked up to find Nora.

Her face looked crestfallen. "I'm sorry, Henry. This is all my fault. It was my idea to come here, and it's been a waste." She took a few steps toward him.

"We knew it was a long shot." He moved to cross the divide between them.

Rocks fell from above their heads, bouncing until they rested at Henry's feet. Nora had jumped back, her hand on her chest. They both looked at each other before shielding their eyes and squinting up to see what had caused the disturbance. In between the fir trees, so tall the tops weren't visible, and the rock wall, the faces of mountain goats looked down at them, on a perch at least twenty feet above their heads.

"I can't even see where they can stand," Nora exclaimed in a hushed voice. "That's a sheer vertical drop."

Henry simply allowed himself the pleasure of watching for a moment as the goats moved higher. "That's because they can find the tiniest rocky crags that are imperceptible to us. Their hooves spread apart, incredibly flexible, with little stabilizers on each one. And in the middle of each hoof, the leathery pads work like suction pads on the rocks. It's amazing all the built-in safety gear they have for their habitat. God's design always impresses me."

"When we were little, my sister used to think the mountain goats were actually unicorns. The way they could jump and look like they were flying from rock to rock."

And just like that, the mention of her sister, reminded him of drugs and the stakes they were dealing with. He wasn't there to spend time with Nora. He turned to look at the scene of the crime once more. "I'd always imagined if I were in charge of the case, we'd have found the killer by now. And instead, he's been here all along and has killed another guide."

"We don't know that. We only know that the cases are connected. If it is the same killer, then we could rule out Zach as a suspect for good. He wasn't around here back then."

Henry trudged forward without commenting. If he looked at the case with fresh eyes, who'd been around at the time of Tommy's murder that would have the means and opportunity to shoot Dexter? "Come on," he finally said. "We need to go if we're going to have time to get the drugs."

If he couldn't find the killer, the least he could do was keep Nora safe. But to do that would likely mean the death of her aunt's company and keeping her off the river. Would the realization that his help was worth nothing be the final nail in the coffin of their relationship?

"What's your plan for getting out of here?" he finally asked, eyeing the rotting log six feet away.

"Boarding that rotten log certainly won't work. The only way out is floating down the river. Feet first, just like you'd do if you'd fallen out of the raft. We'll just need to choose our currents wisely."

"You were right. I didn't want to know." There had to be a better way. He racked his brain for other solutions and came up empty. He was failing her again. He couldn't even come up with a way to keep her safe without the risk of killing them both.

ELEVEN

Henry stared at the churning waters below. "You want me to do *what*?"

"It's the only way, Henry." She pointed to the opposite side of the boulder that had almost killed him. "Look. There's no undertow here. If we hit the right current, we can get to the next stop relatively quickly. It's not that far. If the rain hasn't interfered, we only have to endure one very minor rapid. If you do what I say—without question—we should get to Bobby and Carl quick as a flash." She ripped off her life jacket and removed her splash jacket. "You'll need to take off your splash jacket, as well. I'm glad you dressed properly this time, or I'd be worried about hypothermia."

"I don't understand. Why do you need my jacket?"

She demonstrated instead of answering. With a series of knots, she fashioned her splash jacket into a miniature pillow of sorts and then put her life jacket back on over her wet suit. "You'll want something to hang on to. Let your life jacket do the rest, but this will help you balance and keep you from flailing your arms and legs."

The more she explained the plan, the faster his heart

pumped. Flipping upside down in a kayak was sounding pretty good in comparison. "Even if we can make it there, they can't fit us in their kayak."

"Well, if we straddle—"

"You've got to be joking," he said, handing over his splash jacket.

She grinned and began tying his jacket with the same tight knots. "Sorry. I couldn't resist. We can hope for the unlikely event that Bobby caught our raft, but Carl has a satellite radio, right? He can at least call for another boat to get to us. That take-out should be easy for another raft to reach. Or other options will present themselves."

Henry eyed her. "You would make me take the kayak with Carl while you and Bobby ride the top of the kayak?"

"It would be hard to paddle, and we'd probably sink, so no." She pointed to the sky. "If we don't get a move on, it'll be nightfall before someone could reach us."

That would mean spending the night outside. "That's the only part that doesn't sound so bad." The temperature would drop a good thirty degrees in the middle of the night. "Except we're both soaked, and it's illegal, even for me, to build a fire on this land."

She clicked her harness and flashed a dazzling smile his way that doused him with a feeling of courage. "I know you've struggled with a fear of water the past few years. After your belt got stuck, that probably hasn't changed. But I think you're doing amazing." She reached over as if to pat him on his back, except her palm gave his back a good shove.

The slippery rock offered no friction and he launched

off the rock as if on a waterslide. He dropped ten feet in the air before his feet slapped the water. The water rushed over his head, but he bobbed up as fast as he'd dropped. Nora popped up beside him, her teeth already chattering from the cold.

She reached for his hand even as the stream grabbed them and rushed them forward. "Just pretend you've fallen out of a raft." She took shallow, rapid breaths, her lips already turning a darker shade.

Henry felt sure his must have seemed bluer as she cast a concerned glance at his face. "I don't think pretending I've fallen out of a boat helps keep me calm."

She grinned and he tried to keep his fingers from holding on to her hand too tightly. "Fair enough, but remember, feet forward, following the downstream. Don't try to stand, even if the water is shallow or the river calms."

A wave swept over their heads. Henry wiped his face with his free hand, refusing to let Nora go. He didn't need to be told not to stand, especially after getting stuck in a crevice. She also didn't need to remind him to keep his feet high. Boulders were hidden below the surface.

She raised her chin and continued her safety lecture. "Knees up. Try to keep your feet as close to the surface… I know you know these things, but in a stressful situation, it can help to voice them as reminders. For both of us."

"I suppose I deserve that after diving in after the raft."

She eyed him, her blue lips parted. "Why do you

always assume I'm trying to tell you 'I told you so'? That's not what I was doing. I was *trying* to be helpful, Henry McKnight."

He could feel her fingers pulling from his ever so slightly. "Okay, okay. That's not what you were doing." Her face relaxed ever so faintly, even though her teeth still chattered. He did have a tendency to assume people were trying to control him or to criticize him, but in his defense, that was often true in his life. He'd forgotten that, for all of Nora's supposed easy-going nature, the moment *she* thought someone was trying to control her or had misjudged her, she turned into a stubborn, immovable spitfire. It didn't make sense why he missed that so much.

"Why are you smiling like that?"

"No reason." He fought against a laugh.

She eyed him. "Why do I feel like I'm missing the joke?"

"I was remembering how fierce you can be."

She pursed her lips. "Well, don't forget it. We're entering another canyon."

Walls on either side engulfed them, offering no sign of any banks to climb out upon. "Stay to the right, close to the wall. That's the safest current. Remember to breathe," she added, her voice gentle as they bobbed along the calmer waves.

Her eyes flickered above him. "Henry, look."

The terror returned to his gut. It took all his willpower to look away from what lay ahead to the rock face above him. A line of mountain goats dotted the wall. From his vantage point, they appeared to be standing in midair, as if their fur must have just stuck to the side of the cliffs.

"Looks like they found their way." She lifted her free hand and pointed. "Hopefully, we will find ours, too."

There, two stragglers—the goats they'd seen back at the site, if he had to guess—were rushing effortlessly across the sheer rock wall to join the rest of the herd.

The sound of a snapped branch sent a shiver up Henry's neck. Surely it was just the wind. But the mountain goats seemed spooked, as well. They all took off at unbelievable speed, disappearing over the cliff edge.

"I wonder what—"

A bullet hit the rock wall and sprayed debris over them. Nora let go of his hand, instinctively covering her face as she screamed. Henry reached for the gun on his waist he no longer had and fought not to lower his legs. On the opposite side of the ravine, a gunman perched on the top of the cliff, a rifle aimed in their direction. A bullet splashed the water a foot to his right. Too close. The gunman had them trapped. They had nowhere to run or hide.

Except under water. *No, anything but that, please, Lord.* An idea hit him over the side of the head. "Nora, how is the current next to the other cliff side? Any undertows?"

She looked over. "Risky but should be—"

A bullet hit his helmet. The force flung him back as the sound of Nora's scream pierced the air. He felt her fingers dig into his wrist and drag him closer. "The bullet hit your helmet. Come on!" Her voice shook. "Swim parallel before we have more boulders. Now!"

Henry's brain felt like it was still rattling around his skull, but he reached up to find a foam edge where a chunk of the helmet was missing. He didn't need to be told again. She tugged on his arm and released. He kicked, careful to keep his feet up high, and strained to move toward the opposite rock face even as the stream pressed them forward. Another bullet kicked up a splash of water too close to his hand for comfort.

Just past the halfway point across the river, Nora twisted and pointed her feet up. "We can't go farther but…" She pointed with her left hand, reaching with her right to grasp his hand.

He couldn't quite reach her but kicked his feet forward, trying to understand. Instantly he spotted the churning water near the rock face. Another undertow. The bullets had stopped, though. He looked up. They were in a shadow now. The cliff was so steep, they'd passed the point where the gunman could see them.

A fistful of water sloshed into his mouth as an unexpected wave slapped his face. But even if the gunman couldn't get them now, he'd clearly been waiting for them. And if he'd shot at them, then there was a good chance he'd shot at Bobby and Carl. The waves bounced more violently, interrupting his train of thought. They were rounding a bend.

"We need to be on the other side if we're going to get our chance to get the package." Nora pointed ahead. "Henry, there's no kayak. I'm worried… Bobby?" The fear in her voice spiked his adrenaline. But what could he do without gun, radio or boat? He'd never felt so helpless in his life.

* * *

Nora splayed her arms and legs wide, which only slowed her speed for half a second, but it was enough to get close enough to grab Henry's foot. They needed to be side by side to get back across the river to the site. "This is the hard part."

Henry barked a laugh. "Let me guess. Another plan? I'm not sure I want to know." He looked over his shoulder. "I think we might be past the shooter's vantage point."

"We have other problems now. We're coming up on the take-out site fast. There are several smaller creeks that dump into the river here." She flashed him a sheepish grin. "I forgot that the river is going to rise fast here. And there's only one place that's safe to approach the bank without worrying about an undertow." On a boat, it would be different, but in the water, the risk level jumped exponentially. *I really need Your wisdom and guidance now, Lord.*

Henry gave a resolute nod. "How do we get to that one place?"

"The moment we round the bend, there's a small waterfall to our left, off the rock face. Don't take time to look at it. It produces a crosscurrent only for a moment. We need to use that to our advantage."

She squinted at the area twenty feet from the bank. "See that floating branch up ahead? We're going to need it." The confidence he had in her threatened to break Nora's concentration. She couldn't let him down, but she also couldn't do it on her own, a thought that terrified her. "I don't think I can swim fast enough, even with the cross current, to get across to the branch before we pass it, as much as I try. I've got endurance, not speed."

"Then let me try, Nora."

She remembered all the kayak races they used to enjoy before his accident, but there was no time for reflection. "When I say go, I need you to swim as hard as you can and get on top of the branch."

His lips had turned a purplish shade, but his cheeks were still flushed. "I'm not leaving you behind!"

She twisted, frantically released the throw bag, and pulled out the rescue rope, still gripping the end. Her fingers trembled with the cold as she fought to weave it through the sleeves of her life jacket and knot it at the front.

"I'm not exactly at my peak condition, Nora."

"We've got a better chance together than separately, and we're running out of time. We've got one shot." She pressed her shoulder into his, kicking her left leg out to keep them away from the undertow against the rock face.

She grabbed the current and they slid around the sharp angle of the south-facing rock wall. The soft rumble of the thin waterfall just around the corner stirred up mist. "Go. Now!"

She shoved him with as much strength as she could muster, also flipping over and kicking, doing her best to follow him. Her muscles were spent already and so cold. Her brain told her limbs to move faster and faster, but yet they reacted like they were in quicksand.

Henry seemed to be struggling as well, but he was already six feet ahead of her. She fought to lift her head high enough to pull in a breath before a wave slapped her helmet, veering her off course. The rope tugged. She rolled sideways, the pull of the water twisting her despite her forceful kicks.

"Nora!"

The rope tugged again, and she looked down to see the knot unraveling, loosening. She grabbed the rope with one hand. A wave sloshed over her head and she fought against the conflicting currents, desperate to keep hold of the rope.

She launched forward at an unbelievable speed, no longer fighting, but sliding under water, almost like she was flying. She lifted her head up and pulled in a greedy breath, only to feel Henry's hands gripping the top of her life jacket. He lifted her onto the tree branch, much thicker in diameter and longer in length than she'd guessed. As soon as her stomach hit the rough bark, she wriggled her way to sitting, bouncing the log precariously on one end, but Henry leaned the opposite way, ensuring it'd stay afloat.

"I knew you could do it," she whispered, trying to give her lungs and heart a chance to catch up.

He panted, his chest heaving with the effort of trying to catch his breath. "Failure wasn't an option. Now what?"

"Your legs face north. Mine will face south. Our feet will have to act like oars." She loved the river, but if she could go a day without having to dip a body part into frigid waters, that would be great. "Ready?"

She gave out commands, straining her abdominals, as she had to lean backward in an awkward move to make her legs forceful enough to mimic a paddle. The log soared across the water, keeping them from the danger of an undertow, and smacked against the sand.

She rolled head-over-heels, falling flat onto her back on the ground. Henry had managed to stay upright, facing the log. He offered his hand and pulled her upright. "Thanks for saving my life." She brushed the sand off her legs, which would likely be covered in bruises by nightfall from all the trauma of the day.

Henry stared deeply into her face, his eyes full of emotion, as if trying to hold back a secret.

"Are you okay?"

"Yes." He blinked and nodded, then turned away, scanning the empty bank. "Let's see if Carl and Bobby are here."

"The gunman—"

"I prefer to stay positive. Besides, the shooter seemed to have it in for me instead of you this time. There's a chance this has become personal and the others aren't in danger."

His words shot fear straight to her heart, but he wasn't wrong. Not once had a bullet come her way even though she'd been just as much in the shooter's sights as Henry. In fact, so much so, she had made herself take a good look as she'd swum to the other side.

"He had on a face covering, like the other two incidents, but we both know how common those masks are. This guy had a different build than Dexter's murderer, I'm sure of it. He was more tall and wiry."

Henry raised an eyebrow, his skepticism evident. "When adrenaline hits the—"

She folded her chilled arms across her chest. "Don't make me prove everything I see all over again."

His face went slack, like when he was trying to hide his surprise, and she knew he was finally listening. "Dexter's murderer was average height and slim. I know that's nothing specific," she added hastily, seeing his mouth open. "But the shooter who went after us at the bank had broad shoulders, a more athletic build. Still slim, but almost like he was wearing shoulder pads. More like the man who shoved me down in the lodge. The guy who shot at us just now was tall and wiry."

Henry's jawline pulsed, either from trying to keep his teeth from chattering or grinding his teeth together. She used to kiss his jaw when he'd tense up like that. Nora swung her gaze to the trees, blinking rapidly at the unexpected thought. The cold had frozen a little too many brain cells, that was all. "What if they aren't here?" she asked. "What do we do?"

"Honestly, I don't know." He tipped his head. "I'm not looking forward to going down the river without a raft again."

"That's not an option." She took a deep breath. "The rapids after this are too intense to float without a boat. And if, somehow, we missed Sangster Creek and the final take-out—they both have small windows—then we'd find ourselves in the final canyon."

"A set of rapids every mile and the dreaded Garnet Rapids."

"And Perry warned me about a boulder the size of an SUV right in the middle of our normal route. I was going to check it out to see how to avoid a high-side, but I wouldn't be comfortable trying without the best gear."

"Okay, I get it. We might have to camp out here." Henry reached for the side of his waist. He was missing his gun. His eyes drifted across the river. "Let's get under cover. It would take the gunman a long journey to get off the top of the cliff and over here, but we better not take any chances. Especially if we're dealing with multiple people."

"If Bobby and Carl are fine, they'll have radios. They'll call it in. At least search and rescue can reach us at this site." The breeze blew and she fought against a shiver. "There's a chance we won't have to spend the night, if they're fast. I could really do with a proper cup of tea right now." She ventured a glance at the sun, hovering over the west end of the treetops.

She turned back to see Henry's lips twitch. His lips lost and he coughed a laugh.

"What? What's so funny?"

"A proper cup?"

"Well, it just sounds silly when you say it," she said, fighting back her own laugh. "Okay, I admit, maybe I'm watching too many British shows. I find the accent and pacing to be soothing."

"It might be the tea you're having while you watch it."

She trudged after him but didn't comment. She'd never thought about the chamomile being the reason. She'd been fond of British dramas ever since her mom would come home on Sunday afternoons, her only time off, and want to watch one on PBS. Maya'd had no interest, but Nora had fond memories.

The moment she stepped into the shadows, goose bumps erupted over Nora's arms and legs. Their brief moment of levity vanished along with the warmth the light had provided.

"Carl? Bobby?" Henry called out. His voice seemed strained, as if he didn't want to use his normal volume. Nora wondered if he was afraid to give the gunman a hint about their precise location. Sound carried rapidly between the canyon walls.

He focused on the ground, most likely looking for traces of footprints. The only ones Nora spotted were her own, though.

"The least we can do is retrieve the drugs while we're here, so we're ready when the rescue team comes for us." Henry eyed her. "You still remember where you hid it?"

She fought against rolling her eyes. "I'll see to it."

He half-heartedly nodded and stepped between two trees. "I'll look for any signs of the guys." He stiffened as the trees twenty feet away rustled so violently that it couldn't be an animal unless they were dealing with a cougar or bear. Henry kept his eyes forward and gestured intensely with his left hand, low to the ground. The message was clear. *Go hide.*

Nora hesitated but rounded the boulders where she'd hidden the drugs in the first place. She squatted, unsure she wanted to pull out the drugs until Henry was sure the area was safe. She moved the rock blocking the log and spotted the tiniest bit of red inside. Still safe and—

"Nora?"

She started and spun around. Behind her, Bobby stood, eyes narrowed. "What are you doing here? I've been worried sick."

Nora's breath hitched, wanting to ask him the same question. Had she misjudged Bobby all along? How was it that he'd suddenly appeared so close to where the drugs had been found?

"Stranded," she answered.

"I figured that much, but how'd you get here? I saw your raft float past us. I wanted to keep going down the river until we could get a cell signal to call for help, but Carl—" His voice shook with a level of frustration Nora rarely witnessed from Bobby. "There's something off about that guy. He barely says two words, but then I'm all alone with him and he acts like he's the sheriff himself. Says we need to stay on schedule for stops, but he doesn't even let me land at the safest pullout to get to them."

He pointed behind him. "I never knew there was a path back here. Did you?"

Nora looked over his shoulder. "There's not."

"That tiny space between the boulders. If you step in sideways, it opens up into a bigger path and takes you along the rock face to Boulder Creek. Ironically."

She stepped away from the log where she'd hidden the drugs. "Carl knew about this path?" The news seemed troubling. Carl knew the river better than she did? He'd been so quiet. Too quiet, maybe. "So you don't have a cell or radio signal?"

"No. I'm sure once I get past the cliffs—"

"We're definitely going to need you to call for help. Henry and I can't get off the river without another boat. Is Carl still in there?" She threw a thumb over her shoulder. At his nod, her gut twisted.

"He said he was supposed to pick up something."

Her mouth went dry. Carl was trying to find the drugs without them. And Bobby hadn't mentioned anyone shooting at them. She needed to warn Henry.

"Hold up one second." She turned around, stepped out of her hiding place, and wove through the trees, headed for the area where Henry had been. Two male voices in a relatively heated exchange led her the rest of the way.

"No need to get worked up. I think it's fair to say it's my turn to take over this investigation." Carl's voice carried through the leaves just as Nora stepped past a bush. She spotted Henry's back and Carl's hardened eyes, fists on his waist, just above his gun holster. *It's my turn.* Her breath hitched at his words.

He'd said those three words to Dexter. Right before he'd murdered him. The certainty shot electricity through her veins. Carl's eyes lifted, moving past Henry's shoulder and connecting with Nora's. She tried to relax her face into a forced smile, as if she suspected nothing, but his eyebrows jumped and his eyes flickered with recognition.

Maybe she was reading into things and Carl didn't realize she'd recognized him. "Hi," she said nonchalantly, racking her brain for ideas on how to buy time. She needed to communicate, to let Henry know. "You guys find the drugs yet?"

Henry spun around, his brow furrowed in confusion. Carl's hand moved to his gun. She was out of time and options.

"He's the killer!" She was too little, too late. Carl's arm lifted, his eyes steadily aimed at her.

"Bobby! Run for help!" she screamed at the top of her lungs, praying she'd given Henry enough warning to duck for cover, as well.

TWELVE

Henry spun on one foot back in the direction of Carl. His brain struggled to connect the pieces. But a gun in the man's hand, pointed at Nora, circumvented all thought. Henry's hand balled into a fist. He twisted and slammed his knuckles into the man's jaw with enough force Henry cried out in pain with the contact. He'd deal with potential broken fingers later.

The gun went off. Carl stumbled backward. Henry allowed himself a quick glance, confirming the bullet hadn't hit Nora. "Nora, run!" Carl still had the gun in his hand. They weren't out of danger yet, and Henry didn't have anything to fight back with except the good fifty pounds he had on the man.

Carl's back hit a tree trunk, but he righted himself to standing as he raised his arm to shoot again. Henry ducked low and dove. The top of his head hit the deputy squarely in the ribs. They slid sideways to the ground. Rocks and thorny stems pricked Henry's legs and arms as he fought to flip Carl over onto his back before the man could fire again or hit him with the gun.

More gunshots rang out. Except, they were in the

distance. The two men stilled, and Carl's face transformed into a sneer. "Bobby's not going to be calling anyone for help."

A blurry wave of brown flashed in Henry's peripheral vision before a sick cracking noise reached his ears. In front of him, Carl crumpled. Behind him, Nora stood, trembling as a thick branch fell from her hands. She reached for Henry, pulling him upright.

"I told you to run, Nora."

"You don't always get to be the boss of—"

Carl growled. They both turned to see him on all fours, the gun still in his hand, preparing to get back up.

"*Now* we should run." Nora sprinted off in the opposite direction of the bank. Henry almost screamed at her to follow him, but he kept on her heels. Carl yelled and launched three bullets through the air, but they seemed like wild ones fired more out of rage than precision. Nora ducked behind a massive boulder right into a dead end. If she'd thought they could hunker down and hide, and he wouldn't find them, she was sorely—

She darted sideways through a precariously thin space between a boulder and the rock wall. "Come on," she whispered.

Henry pursed his lips and followed. At least it would be a hiding place. Except, as they sidestepped into the shadows and ignored the disturbingly large webs above their heads, the opening widened. A natural but thin, rocky path between boulders and the rock face wall seemed to lead to an intersection of creek and river. If they could make it there, it was possible they could run away on the banks of the creek.

Nora twisted, beckoning with her hand for him to move faster. "Hurry! Carl knows about this path."

The momentary hope vanished in an instant. Carl was only five years younger than him but seemed lithe and fit. There was no way they could outrun him. Especially since Carl had a radio, a gun and apparently more gunmen waiting for his orders.

Nora tripped on a rock and fell, crying out. He rushed forward to help. Carl would know instantly where they were. *Help me find a weapon, please.* David's slingshot and rocks instantly came to mind—the story of how he'd defeated Goliath—but Henry had never been a good pitcher. He'd never so much as played Little League. He was, however, prepared to take a bullet if that meant Nora could get to safety. He leaned over, grabbed her waist and helped her to a standing position.

The bushes ten feet ahead shifted.

Nora gasped. "Henry, what—?"

A hole in the rock face appeared where the bushes had parted. How was he supposed to protect her when there was danger coming at them from every side?

"Get in here. Now," a female voice whispered.

Henry squinted to see the face of a woman, who resembled Nora, peeking out of the shadows. The same dark hair pulled back in a braid confirmed his suspicions.

"Maya?" Nora said weakly. "Is that really you?"

The sound of shifting rock propelled him into action. Carl would barrel right around the corner in seconds at this rate. Henry would rather take his chances with Nora's sister than the gunman, but both possibilities seemed fraught with danger. Nora, however, seemed too stunned to move. Henry placed his hands on her waist once more, lifting her up and over the next boulder. That seemed to stir her awake, and she launched into the rock face opening as Henry followed closely behind.

Maya released the bushes, which, upon closer examination, were attached to a net on the backside with long strands of wild grasses running through them for better coverage. She dropped a green canvas veil behind her and they were enveloped with darkness. "Be quiet," she whispered. "He doesn't know exactly where I am, but he knows the entrance is somewhere around here."

Henry's gut dropped. Right when Nora had finally seemed to forgive him for his part in the divide of their sisterly relationship, why had Maya needed to show up? She was clearly part of the mess they were in. Were they walking into a bigger trap?

Nora took shallow breaths of the cold, musty air. Her bones vibrated and her hair felt as if it was starting to freeze instead of dry after their swim in the rapids. A dim light appeared in front of Maya. Nora held a hand to her heart. "You were in town, then. All along?" Her voice cracked ever so slightly. All those years of pain and worry and loneliness, and her sister could have stopped by at any time. Did Maya hate her so much she couldn't have even tried to heal the divide between them?

"Follow me." Maya shuffled along a dusty path with rocks on either side. She turned a sharp corner and flipped a switch. Lightbulbs rigged by electric wiring draped precariously along the ceiling sprang to life. They were standing on a long, inclined straight path made of metal grates, like an enormous ramp. "We can probably talk now, if we're not too loud."

"What are you doing here?" Nora asked.

Maya raised an eyebrow and popped her hip out to the side, the same sassy move she used to do whenever she didn't like Nora's input. "Saving your life. Obviously." Her brows dropped low over her eyes. "I was assured you would never be in danger, so the deal is clearly off."

"Who? Who assured you? Carl?" Henry asked.

Maya pursed her lips but only gave him a cursory glance before addressing Nora again. "I see you two are still together."

Fire sparked in Nora's chest and she embraced the heat and stepped closer to Maya. "When you slammed the door on our relationship, you lost the right to comment on my love life. And what are you now?" She thrust her hands out, gesturing to the tunnel. "A smuggler?"

Maya's eyes glistened for half a second before she blinked hard and turned away. "At the moment, I'm your rescuer, so I think you can leave your high-and-mighty comments for someone who cares."

A flood of regrets cascaded over her, so much so, she could hardly pull in a breath. She'd failed. Nora reached for her arm. Maya flinched but didn't move away. A cry caught in Nora's throat, as she pulled Maya into her arms. "You're my sister," she whispered.

Her mom had told her to take care of her sister, and

here Maya was—obviously involved in drugs or worse. Part of Nora didn't want to know. She wanted to pull Maya out of this hole in the literal ground, wash her up and get her back on track. Whatever it took. But instead of the big sister lecture on the tip of her tongue, she pulled in a breath, catching hints of vanilla and coconut. The familiar scent of Maya's favorite shampoo eased her heart. At least some things stayed the same. "I missed you," Nora said instead.

"And sharing your soaked shirt with me." Maya pushed her back, half-heartedly but with a soft smile, though her eyes were downcast. Her satellite radio burst with static and she dialed it down before words could be heard. "The less you know, the better. Come on. Let's get you out of here."

"You know I can't agree to that," Henry said softly. "I can't pretend I never saw or heard anything, but I want to help you, Maya. Honestly, I do. I know I acted rashly the, uh, last time I saw you."

The sister Nora used to know appeared for a split second before all emotion seemed to disappear and Maya's spine straightened. "Like I said, we need to keep moving."

"This—" Henry gestured in front of him "—can't be the life you wanted."

Maya crossed her arms over her chest and scowled at them both. "Ganging up on me again? Nora, you always were so judgmental. Drugs help people, okay? They want them. I help supply them. I have a good life."

"In this—"

Maya held up a hand. "I only work here in the spring

and then I'm free to go and do whatever I want the rest of the year. Wherever I want. Which is away from judgmental people like you."

"Do you take drugs, too?" Nora fought to act nonchalant. If her sister wanted nonjudgmental, she would deliver.

She shrugged. "I don't, personally. I prefer to provide a service for a lucrative income. Give the people what they want. No one gets hurt." Maya started ever so slightly. If she hadn't known her, Nora wouldn't have seen that Maya had realized the mistake in her words.

"I almost died," Nora said softly. "More than once. I've been shot at. Bobby got shot at today. I don't know if he's—" She placed a hand over her mouth, trying her best to hold back her fear.

"Bobby?" Maya's armor cracked. "They shot at him?" She blinked rapidly. "Did you ever think that maybe I didn't visit, didn't get back in touch, because it's the only way to keep you safe?"

Nora stopped midstep. "What is that supposed to mean?"

Maya shook her head. "Forget it." She moved forward, but there was no way Nora would let a statement like that go.

"One of your aunt's guides was murdered last week," Henry said before Nora had formed her next question. "Dexter—"

Maya trudged ahead, following the string of lights. "Yeah, I knew about him, but that wasn't part of the plan. Carl wasn't supposed to—"

"Is he in charge of all this?" Henry interjected. "Deputy Carl Alexander?"

Maya spun and rolled her eyes at Nora as if to say, *Can you believe this guy?* She blew a thin line of air out past her lips. "He acts like it sometimes. But no, he's not in charge. He's just a jerk, though I heard his hand was forced."

"By who?"

"It's better you don't know."

"Are you in charge?"

Maya barked a laugh. "I may be important, but would I really *choose* to become an expert in old mining tunnels if I were the boss? Give me a little credit."

"Is this related to Tommy?" Henry asked. "Did he die for the same reason?"

"Don't ask me any more questions," Maya said. Her statement signaled an order, but her voice sounded like a plea. For all Maya's bravado, Nora's heart twisted with compassion.

She reached for her sister's hand. They both stopped and finally made eye contact. "What do you mean that you've been protecting me?"

Maya's nose wrinkled in the way it used to when trying to decide something. Nora fought against impatience and waited.

"I got in this for the money, the freedom," Maya said with a lift of her chin. "I know you could never understand, but I wanted something for myself. Haven't you ever wanted that? I mean, we didn't even get our own rooms growing up. Ever. Aunt Linda was so worried about seemingly giving us preferential treatment, she had us sleeping in the lodge with the other employees!"

"You have to keep in mind Aunt Linda never even knew Mom. She didn't even know she had a half sister when she was asked to take us in." The tendency to defend Aunt Linda's choices took Nora by surprise. She didn't want to admit that she'd fought carrying the same grudge for many years.

Maya threw a thumb into her chest. "*I've* been able to go places I've always wanted, Nora."

Nora tried her best to smile but couldn't.

Maya's smile also dropped. "It wasn't as much fun when I didn't have anyone to tell, so I tried once to get... I did try. But..."

"They threatened to hurt Nora. Didn't they?" Henry's harsh voice broke the tenderness of the moment. "And your aunt?"

Maya pulled back, releasing Nora's hand. "Listen, it's safer if you stop asking questions. I'll get you out of here, and you can do what you want. Just don't mention me as part of any of it, if you want to keep Nora and Aunt Linda safe."

Nora twisted to gauge Henry's reaction. Maya had directed her words at him but turned to Nora as if to confide. "You can't trust anyone. I don't know who is on the payroll, but I know you're being watched."

Nora's mouth dropped. "Is there one from the US Forest—"

"I don't know who all is involved, I told you." Her eyes flashed. "You mentioned Tommy. I don't know any details about that, either. Promise me you'll stop asking questions, Nora."

"You at least know some of the payroll," Henry interrupted.

"It's not safe to talk about." Maya eyed Henry. "For all I know, you're in on it."

"How 'bout we remedy that, and I get you set up with some witness protection? While I protect your sister. If Nora lets me know your aunt's whereabouts, I can make some calls and get her safe, as well."

Maya turned, looked ahead, and placed a hand on her forehead. "I need to focus. I can't take you my normal route." They came to an intersection where the tunnels split three ways. Maya stretched her chin forward. "Did you hear that?"

Nora strained her ears. Footsteps echoed through the tunnels.

"Carl found the entrance." Maya turned to them. "I have an idea, but you're going to have to trust me," she whispered.

Nora almost groaned aloud. How could they do that?

Henry shivered, standing in the darkness. Maya killed the lights, flipping a switch at the intersection of the mine tunnels. A moment later, a bright spotlight shone from a headlamp he didn't realize she'd been wearing. She beckoned them forward.

"I don't like using this tunnel," she whispered. "There are some vertical shafts that drop hundreds of feet farther down. We'll stop way before that, but it gives me the creeps." The tunnel they'd entered wasn't nearly as modern—which was saying something—as they sidestepped trash in the form of discarded lanterns, a pile of seemingly old dynamite, a broken shovel and a four-foot wooden ladder. Pebbles and a few rocks the size of baseballs littered the path, as well.

Maya shifted her headlamp beam before he could look at the ceiling to judge the likelihood of being buried alive in a cave-in. They were only about forty miles from a known fault line. He hoped, if the tunnels had stood the test of time after so many earthquakes, that this one was sturdy. The moment they passed a precarious beam, Maya shifted her back against the wall and gestured for them to do the same.

Playing hide-and-seek from an officer five years his junior went against the fiber of Henry's being, but Nora's safety—and therefore her sister's—took priority. The rattle of metal echoed. Maya's headlamp went dark. Henry remembered his feet causing the same sound on the metal grates. Carl had to be roughly a hundred feet from the intersection of tunnels. Would the deputy turn around without light helping him lead the way?

There were thousands of abandoned mines in Idaho, many undocumented. In his short time as a ranger, they'd had one off-road vehicle unintentionally discover a nearby vertical mineshaft. Those types of hidden mines were the scariest. Thankfully, they'd rescued the two individuals without serious injury, though they'd been trapped for two days before the search party had found them. Henry's throat tightened at the thought of being trapped inside a cold, damp environment for days.

Finding and entering the locations of discovered

mines into a state database was one of the priorities of his job, but this particular set of tunnels was quite extensive, and he was sure they were not all on record yet. Copper or silver mines would be his guess. Whoever Maya's boss was had likely discovered these mines and worked very hard to keep it a secret, from what Henry could tell. Otherwise, he and other nature enthusiasts would've discovered one of this magnitude by now. Maybe every exit and entrance had been camouflaged. He just prayed it would be easier to find ways out than in.

Nora's breath shuddered next to him. Their shoulders touched, providing the only side-by-side warmth in the freezing tunnel. He adjusted his stance so he'd be ready to pounce if needed. Their hands brushed and it felt like electricity rushed up his spine, sharpening his senses. He bent his head and whispered into her damp hair, "Are you okay?"

She turned to him before he pulled away and her lips brushed against his cheek. He felt paralyzed for a second, the memory of their past kisses heating his neck. "I'm fine, but he has a gun, Henry," she whispered so softly he could barely hear the words. "He has a gun and you don't. Please don't try anything."

He squeezed her hand to indicate it would be all right, but he had to ignore the instinct that told him to say, *Actually, I have two guns—Ka and Pow*, while flexing each arm. His older brother and he had always made jokes like that. His brother had followed his father's path as a lawyer, ensuring his father's disappointment in Henry's choice of career, but they'd recently made peace. "If he's smart at all, he won't shoot with the big risk of a ricochet in here."

A small splash of water… Henry remembered barely missing the puddle caused by dripping water. Hundreds of small waterfalls in the area and snow on tops of mountains guaranteed leaks inside the tunnel. Judging from the sounds, Carl was likely only twenty feet away. Maybe Carl knew the tunnels better than Maya thought he did. If so, hopefully the man would move on to the most likely path away from them.

From behind them, a phone light washed over the walls. Henry pulled his chin closer to his chest and noticed the loose rocks littering the ground beside his feet. David and Goliath came to mind again, but he didn't have a sling and Carl wasn't a giant. Still, a rock was better than nothing.

Henry squatted and tried to remember where he'd seen the closest baseball-size rock. His fingers brushed the rocks, careful not to shift pebbles and cause sound. More footsteps echoed, moving away. He stayed in the crouch a moment longer, just in case his knees decided to break the silence when he straightened.

The beam of light flashed back into the tunnel, illuminating the tips of Henry's shoes, but also Carl's face and the Taser in his right hand. Henry's biceps were no match against a Taser. He launched himself forward and threw the rock. His aim proved true, at the sound of plastic cracking and Carl's shout of pain. The Taser crashed against the side of the tunnel and the phone light hit the dirt, pointing upward.

Henry vaulted forward. He just needed to get the gun in the deputy's holster before the man grew desperate.

Carl grabbed the stick from his belt and, with a flick of his wrist, the baton extended. Henry froze a moment before making impact, knowing how officers were trained and the pain that little stick could inflict. The light showed the red circle on Carl's knuckles where the rock had left its mark. If Henry could get close enough, he might be able to disarm him.

His nerves fired warnings of the impending sting and pain if he failed, particularly in the leg that had once shattered. Henry held his hands out far enough to not be a risk.

Carl whipped the baton in front of him, as if proving what a threat he could be. "Give me the drugs."

"We don't have them."

The deputy took a step closer, and Henry moved back. "Then tell me where they are, and we can call a truce."

Henry almost laughed aloud at the implication he'd be so gullible. "Again, I can honestly say I don't know."

"Wrong answer." Carl lunged, waving the baton in an arc over his head.

Henry jumped, but gained more height than distance. The snap of the baton crackled close to his ear and made contact with his shoulder. The sting radiated down his spine and through his bones, rattling him. He growled and plowed his head into Carl's stomach, wrapping his arms around the deputy's torso. Carl tried to smack him again, but only the handle of the baton hit Henry's back.

The pain throbbed in his shoulder, almost enough

to cause Henry to release the man, but if he didn't take Carl out now, Nora would be in more danger. He twisted and bent his right arm around Carl's head, pushing it downward while he used his left hand to bend Carl's wrist back until he dropped the baton.

A stomp on Henry's instep loosened his grip. He cried out and Carl pushed him away. One of them must've kicked the phone because the light all but disappeared. Henry took several quick steps back, and Carl ran at him. He raised his arms instinctively to block, but Carl punched him right in the gut.

He lost his breath for seconds that felt more like minutes as he stumbled backward, hoping the space between them would give him a beat before Carl attacked again. But as he stepped farther into the darkness, he realized it'd be best to draw Carl deeper, away from the intersection of the three tunnels. Hopefully, Maya would take the opportunity to get Nora out and far away while she could.

His foot reached something smooth and firm. He took another step and felt the ground wobble ever so slightly, but it was likely wood panels instead of the metal grates used in the other tunnel for sturdier flooring. Carl lunged for him, and a rush of cold air hit him at the same time Carl's fist made contact with his chin. His skull rattled from the impact of teeth against teeth at his jaw shutting with unusual force.

"Henry!" Nora screamed.

A bright light burst from Maya's headlamp just as Carl aimed another punch at Henry's head. Henry ducked at the last second. The man's knuckle grazed the top of his head, but the force of the punch sailed past him. Carl twisted with momentum and dropped, disappearing from view with a sudden holler.

Terror gripped every muscle as Henry looked down to see a vertical shaft on either side of the precariously thin wooden bridge. Nothing but darkness and cold air swirled below him. Carl had completely disappeared into the abyss.

"Don't move!" Maya yelled.

The bridge vibrated over the open vertical shaft.

"I thought you said there weren't any vertical shafts until much deeper in this tunnel," Henry challenged.

"I misjudged."

So had Carl.

Maya moved to the edge of the shaft and bent her head to shine the light down. Henry forced himself to look again. The only things visible were the wood and rock frames of the seemingly endless pit. He closed his eyes against the sudden onslaught of what-ifs and emotions until his stomach lurched and he questioned his balance. He looked over his shoulder to see the edge of the wooden bridge slip from the ground behind him.

THIRTEEN

Nora rushed forward, arms and hands outstretched.
Maya also lunged, her legs braced in a wide stance.
Henry's eyes widened in the beam of Maya's headlamp
as he jumped.

His toes touched the edge of the rock. His waving
arms flung upward, too far away for her to reach as he
fought to catch his balance. Nora gripped the edge of
his life jacket and Maya grabbed the opposite side and
pulled, squatting for more momentum.

Henry pitched frontward and tripped over another
rock. Dust kicked up in the air and irritated Nora's
throat while Maya and Henry coughed.

"I'd rather not think about what's in the air," Maya
said. "Come on. Let's get out of here."

Nora reached for Henry. "Why didn't you grab our
arms when we tried to help you?"

"And risk taking you down with me? I know you're
strong, but not *that* strong." He tugged her into a hug.
"You still saved me. Thanks for pulling me the rest of
the way."

He bent his head into the embrace and his cheek

brushed against hers. She heard the stress in his uneven breathing and fought to keep her own steady. "How do we make this all stop?" she whispered.

Her sister's light bobbed as she walked away from them. Henry let Nora go and straightened to follow, but her feet wouldn't cooperate. "What about him?" she challenged her sister. "We can't just leave Carl there."

"There's no way he survived, sis. Don't waste any tears on him." Maya's clipped tone bounced off the close walls. "He wasn't a nice man—never was. He embezzled search and rescue funds. That's how he got recruited in the first place. Probably wasn't doing nice things before that."

Maya's statements prompted more questions about Carl. "Is that how you justify your part?" she asked. "You weren't doing bad things before that?"

"I shouldn't have said anything. It's safer that way."

Henry straightened. "Maya, I can't let this go, either. You know that. We need to call this in." He beckoned Nora forward and held her hand until they made it into the intersection where Maya flipped on the electricity to the dangling lightbulbs.

"Do what you want, but I'm not going with you."

"Maya, listen to reason. As soon as we get out of here—with or without your help—this operation is all going to be shut down one way or another. Let Henry help you."

"You don't know who you're dealing with—"

"Then give me the upper hand by explaining it to me," Henry interjected.

Maya stood still, breathing hard for a moment.

"You're right. I know you're right, but you have to promise me not to take this to anyone local or—" her eyes flickered to Nora "—people will get hurt."

"You have my word." Henry's voice dropped almost an octave. "I'll do whatever it takes to keep everyone in your family safe."

Maya stared him full in the face. "A lot of meth is made throughout the forest areas. Then we have the classics coming in from Canada."

"The classics?"

Maya appeared to bristle at Nora's question.

"Heroin, cocaine, you name it. They cross the border by foot then get picked up and taken to the interstate bordering Montana. But before they get to the heavily patrolled areas, they jog over on state highways to Sauvage. From there, our guides take the stuff and any other meth down the river. It avoids all potential patrols.

"Everything is uncut. They leave the drugs at the Sangster Creek site and move on. I come out of my hiding place and hike the tunnels. There's a shortcut soon that'll take me right to Copper City where we cut the drugs and distribute them. From that vantage point, there are many easy options for distribution in the tristate area without detection."

Nora gasped. The abandoned mining town in the middle of nowhere, at the top of a mountain, had very few buildings left, but the ones that were there were historically protected. Schools in the area made field trips there annually.

"We only do it in the spring, sis. No kids are ever in

danger," Maya chided. She apparently still knew Nora well enough to know where her thoughts went.

"They use guides?" Nora asked. "*Our* river guides?"

She shrugged. "It's easy money for them. It helped you get employees, really. It's always been a selective process for those that can keep their mouths shut."

"What's the motivation to stay quiet?" Henry asked.

"Besides money?" Maya asked, as if the answer should've been obvious, until her eyes fell on Nora's gaze.

"Were they worried about their families like you were worried about me?" Nora shook her head. She already knew the answer. "I don't think I could ever thank you for employees like Dexter."

"He was not our typical employee." Maya shrugged. "The point is, the system has always worked. Until Carl got out of hand."

"You're saying you know he was the one who killed Dexter?"

Her eyes widened. "I'm not saying anything."

"What about Tommy?" Nora asked.

"Carl wasn't involved then," Maya admitted.

"Tell me who's in charge, and I'll keep you and your sister safe," Henry repeated.

Maya pointed behind them. "Take that tunnel. At each turn, take the one that goes up instead of down, despite your instincts. When it splits into two with no other choices, go right. That should get you out." She reached for her satellite radio and twisted the dial. Static filled the air, and she nodded to herself as if it was the confirmation she needed. Switching it off, she handed the device to Nora. "The moment you get out, hit that side button and—this is very important, Nora—say that you're going deep and mountainside update in four. Got it?"

Nora repeated the words.

"Good. Our voices sound enough alike, it should buy me enough time." She turned to Henry. "Then you can use the satellite radio on a different channel to get someone to pick you up."

Nora wrapped her hand around her sister's. "You're not coming with us?"

"The only way you're going to keep me safe is if you let me go for now. If they know you're coming back with law enforcement, they'll make this whole place collapse and destroy all those historical buildings before you have a chance, I guarantee it. You'll be hard-pressed to find any evidence."

The back of her neck tightened, remembering the dynamite she'd seen.

Henry folded his arms across his chest and eyed Maya. "How much time we talking?"

"I don't need long at all. You can go ahead and call any law enforcement buddies you want, as long as they aren't local. I'll meet you tonight and tell you everything I know. At the lodge." Maya hesitated. "Nora has to move out first, though."

"What?" Nora slapped a hand over her mouth, shocked she'd been so loud, as her piercing question echoed through the caverns.

Maya shook her head. "It's the only way. I need to

see for myself you're not there. As long as I know you're safe, I'll spill everything I know."

"Where do you expect I'll go?"

"Understood," Henry said over her question. "She'll be protected at an undisclosed location until the threat you're worried about is behind bars. Good enough?"

Maya nodded. "I need to get going and so do you. Nora, be careful." She took off, practically running away down the tunnel.

Nora squeezed the satellite radio tight and turned to face the other tunnels. Without a headlamp, the darkness intensified. She took her phone from her inside wetsuit pocket. Without a cell signal, she knew it would only be useful as a flashlight.

They made their way in silence, following Maya's instructions without discussion. Nora's blood pumped hard and fast. After everything, she was supposed to pack up and move out of the only home she'd ever known on a moment's notice? That was the last straw for her aunt's business. The FBI, or whomever Henry called, would take weeks to collect evidence throughout these mines. Murder and drugs, and apparently dirty cops, would mean a firestorm of media. The travel writer would have to be blind to miss that, even if Nora was permitted to still run the rapids, which she doubted. She lost her balance and her shoulder tipped into Henry.

"Do you trust her?" Henry's voice was soft, punctuated by shallow breathing. The air seemed to get thinner and the walls grew closer. Something dripped ahead in a steady beat.

Nora flinched. Years ago, she would've raised a intense defense for Maya before even considering her true thoughts on the matter. Maya was her sister, her only family, but all her defenses had shattered. "I'd like to think so." She leaned forward to make the incline a little easier on her knees as they climbed. "It's been my job for so long to…" She huffed a breath. "It's going to sound stupid to you."

"Can I take a shot?" He stopped at the top where the paths diverged and put his hands on his head, a trick she'd taught him years ago to help catch his breath quickly. He lowered his arms slowly. "It was your job to keep your sister happy while your mom was working."

Nora nodded. "Yes, but—"

"And by doing so, that made your mom happy. You've worked so hard to make everyone in your life happy, Nora. Even me. But you can't *make* anyone be happy."

Her eyes burned and she blinked back angry, hot tears. "Well, it didn't work anyway. I've lost everyone so far, haven't I? Dad, Mom, you—" Her voice broke and she inhaled sharply, embarrassed to have included him in the list. She pointed to the right and stepped around him, determined to shove the pain further down. She would not crack. She would be strong.

"Nora," he said again, softer, pleadingly, "is that what you thought about me?"

She bit her lip, not ready to turn around to face him. Her heart couldn't take another blow today.

Henry could see his breath as a white cloud. The faster they could get into the sunshine, the better. The mountain peaks were still covered in snow, and even in the summer months, many mines were known to be close to freezing inside. Maybe the cold had addled his brain and that's why his tongue had grown so careless. He'd stepped into the dangerous conversation, so he might as well try to get to the other side. "Like you said, we grew apart, I made mistakes—"

She stopped walking and her shoulders drooped, but she didn't turn around. "We both know you weren't the only one. I…I think it's been easier to pick up other's burdens rather than to figure out what my own are." She shook her head. "I've been so busy taking care of others, sometimes it feels like I don't even know myself."

Henry stepped forward and pulled her into a hug. *He* knew her. He could tell her exactly who she was. But it was like a hand had been placed on his heart, holding him back. Even though it was his instinct to challenge others to rise up and be the best they could be, this seemed like one of those times he needed to check his desires against what God may have in mind for her. He blew out a breath, remained silent, and simply held her in his arms.

If he was honest, he struggled sometimes to be himself. The few times he dropped all the armor in front of Him, though, he became overwhelmed with a sense of freedom and joy. The thought jolted him. Why didn't he go to the Lord more often, then?

Nora lifted her cheek ever so slightly from his chest, her fingers gliding over his forearms. "I think I'm grieving over Maya's choices. I know they're *her* choices, but I hate feeling like I can't help." Her smile wobbled.

"It's probably time to figure out what a healthier relationship with Maya looks like. New boundaries and all. This might be a rough road ahead. And then there's my aunt…"

She stepped away from him, the phone light illuminating the blush in her cheeks. "Well, my hand was about to be forced anyway. Lizzie Hartman and a bunch of the guides decided to move to Frank's company. I can't blame them. The pay is better." She sighed.

He wanted to encourage her, but still fought to stay quiet. Without Maya or her aunt keeping her at the rafting company, would she leave the area?

"I'm afraid of being selfish," Nora said with a sigh. "I want to be the type of person who helps the people I love, but I'm also tired of being taken advantage of. And right now, I'm certain of one thing." She looked into his eyes, searching.

He held his breath for half a second. "What's that?" he whispered.

Her eyebrows jumped as if surprised she'd spoken aloud. "Uh, that I want to get out of this freezing cave before I completely melt down."

He forced a laugh, troubled that despite his resolve, there was a part of him that had started to hope for a new start. Today he'd realized they work better together as a team. And maybe Nora would've been able to see that if not for Maya's reminding her of the rocky times. It served as a reminder for him, as well. They'd lost their chance of a future together long ago, and the faster he accepted that, the better. He turned back to face the never-ending hike in the darkness.

The terrain of the mine shifted and started a sharp decline. Henry shifted in front of her. Her hands gripped his shoulders at the most precarious dips as his shoes barely gripped the ground among the shifting shale. They walked quietly for what seemed like an hour. He kept his eyes directed at the ground, fully conscious of the fact Maya had been mistaken about one vertical shaft. He wouldn't make the same mistake again.

"How did you figure out the boundaries with your parents?" she asked suddenly.

"I think I'm still practicing. I tend to swing the opposite of you. You will bend over backward to rearrange your priorities just to make someone smile, whereas I often mistake the desire for teamwork as people trying to control me."

"You used to be proud of your assertiveness. I volley between doormat and stubborn bull with not much middle ground."

"I was going to say 'guard dog.'"

She laughed. "What?"

"You're usually trying to protect someone else when you get like that."

Nora gasped, and his heart jumped. "What? What is it?"

"I don't want to get my hopes up but..." She clicked the phone off and darkness draped them except a sliver of light. "An exit."

They slid down the remaining rocks and the light engulfed them. Nora held a hand up to block the sun from her eyes, squinting and smiling. Henry hated to hold her back, but he had to be certain. "Please. Wait here for one second."

Her smile vanished. "You're worried it's a trap."

"I'm being cautious. I don't have any way to protect you right now." He found a foothold and vaulted through the opening. Brown and green rolling hills held patches of thick snow and the rest of the expanse was dotted with spruce, fir and lodgepole pines. He turned back to see how the mine had been hidden. The opening reminded him of a whale's mouth, narrow and wide. The sun hit the rocks and produced a green and yellow hue. But he was at such a sharp incline, anyone walking or driving on an easier path would never see the opening.

He reached out a hand and guided Nora outside. She exhaled in relief. "I've never missed the sunshine so much, but it's a little closer to the horizon than I'd expected. We've been gone most of the day."

His throat objected to leaving the humid confines of the tunnels, reminding him of how long it had been since he'd had a glass of water despite hiking for miles. A motor revved in the distance and they both froze, staring at each other for half a beat.

"The radio," she whispered, holding it up with a question in her eyes.

The revving sound grew louder and he spotted a cloud of dust in the distance. He wanted to believe it was a group of friendly ATV drivers, but with snow still on the high hills, they'd need to be pretty determined to venture up this high. Most people waited until July when all signs of snow had disappeared from the mountaintops. He turned around and spotted the summit where Copper City was located. How many hours had they been hiking and stuck in that cave?

He stepped behind a grouping of trees. If the ATVers came around the bend, he and Nora would hopefully be hidden. "Go ahead and call, before they get any closer to overhear."

She swiveled the knob on the sat radio Maya had given her. Rapid-fire, with bursts of static in between, male voices sounded off updates in terms Henry didn't understand. They were using a code of some sort. Nora raised the radio up to her mouth. At the first break of silence, Henry nodded his encouragement.

"Going inside." Her eyes widened and she shook her head. "Sorry, I mean, going deep. Mountainside update in four." She snapped the radio off and clamped her lips closed. "Maya would've never apologized."

He was thinking the same thing, but he reached out his hand with a smile to take the radio. "We're finally in my neck of the woods."

"You know where we are?"

He nodded and shifted the radio function to the text feature. His fingers stilled. Who would he call? If Perry or anyone in the sheriff's office was involved, then Maya had reason to be concerned for Nora's safety. He'd need to tread carefully. And while he didn't trust Maya fully, she had led them out of the mines and given them a way to call for help. He took her assurances to heart that all evidence would be destroyed if he called in the wrong people. The closest FBI office was in Coeur d'Alene. Was that too close? If Carl was on the take, it was possible the drug ring had an FBI officer also on the payroll. Maybe that was the real reason behind Tommy's killer having never been brought to justice.

"Can...can we text Bobby to see if he's okay? I told him to run to get help." The strain around her eyes overwhelmed him. He was ashamed to admit that after the fight with Carl in the tunnel, he'd forgotten about the shots they'd heard on the river. Another set of engines revved nearby, causing them both to still. Without his holster and in the middle of nowhere, his earlier bravado about keeping her safe seemed to drift away with the clouds.

He took a deep breath. "Do you think you're up for more hiking? I know the way back to the highway from here. Once we get a little farther away from whatever is going on here, we'll make some calls."

"Who will you call?"

He'd been hoping she wouldn't ask. "From what Maya told us, whoever is in charge was also here when Tommy was murdered." He reached for her hand as they traversed a path covered in pine needles.

"So that rules out Zach as a likely suspect. Besides, he got injured, so he probably can't pick us up. But Perry—"

"Helped get us the only lead we have. He gave us the lead that the gun used to shoot us from that bank was the same gun used to shoot Tommy."

"But maybe he did that just to throw off our suspicion. He's got broad shoulders like the guy who tried to attack me."

"He's got an athletic build, sure, but an average height." Henry tried to shake off the irritation every time she mentioned Perry's shoulders. "Plenty of guys can match that description. Like me," he added half-heartedly.

"No." She shook her head and stomped forward.

Her reaction gave him pause. "No? No, what?"

"Your shoulders are much broader." She waved a carefree hand over her shoulder. "Never mind."

He fought to ignore how pleased he was with her observation. Before they'd dragged up the past guarding his heart had been easier. Any temptation to flirt or care what she thought would've been far from his mind. He needed that hard edge back now more than ever. Not only for his sake but also to keep her safe. "Nora, whoever comes to pick us up—"

"Call whoever you want. I just want to make sure Bobby is okay." She lifted her chin, a determined gleam in her eyes. "We can pretend we don't know anything. We heard gunshots—we can say that much, right? It doesn't reveal we know all about Maya, Carl and the drugs. So we say the gunshots made us get off the river. We took a trail and got lost."

He cringed and gestured to the left, to a path down the hillside behind the trees. "Maybe skip the last part. I can't admit to getting lost. I'm a ranger."

"Hurts your street cred?" she asked with a laugh.

"Something like that." He nodded, the easy humor they'd shared gone. "We can work on our story on the way down." The words gripped his heart with new meaning. He felt certain that they'd never get a second chance to start their story again.

FOURTEEN

Nora stared at the door in the sheriff's backseat, wondering if it was locked like that when he transferred prisoners. It turned out she and Henry had wasted time arguing about who would pick them up. When they'd gotten far enough away from the revving engines, the only person they could reach was the sheriff himself.

The man had definitely been around since before Tommy had been killed, and as he and Henry discussed the events—an edited version—of the day, she wondered if Henry considered the sheriff a suspect, as well. He certainly was in a powerful position.

"So, we've got two missing men," the sheriff explained. "Perry hasn't been seen since after he dropped Zach off at the urgent care clinic to get a tetanus shot and stitched up—"

"He was hurt that bad?"

"Oh, you know. Nothing worse than you see in a typical whitewater season, but Zach is playing it up as injury in the line of duty. His wife will be spoiling him rotten, mark my words." The sheriff chuckled and shook his head. For a potential suspect, the sheriff sure didn't seem like the type to be a drug lord and a murderer.

"Who's the other missing man?" Henry asked. Nora's gut clenched.

"Bobby Olson, but it's too soon to call out—"

"He was shot at," Nora blurted. "We heard—"

"Every available man went out on the river to look. That is why I'm the only one available to drive you back. But it's too soon to panic. Let's give it a few more hours. I imagine, like you, Bobby probably found his way back to land, and Perry probably got caught up following a lead without a cell signal to check in to his office." He waved at Henry. "You know how these things work. We can't go jumping on assumptions. There's no sign of blood or foul play so far."

There certainly was foul play all day when they were out on the river, but Nora held her tongue. The sheriff pulled up next to Henry's truck in the lodge parking lot. They got out wordlessly, aside from a wave of thanks.

Henry walked alongside her, unusually quiet. "You probably can't wait to get changed and warm," she said.

He focused on the ground. "Something's bothering me, but I can't pinpoint it. Let me get you inside and make sure you're safe. Pack up whatever you need for a few days. I'm going to go pick up a change of clothes, make some calls, and be back here in an hour, before nightfall."

As they stood in the doorway to her room, the only real home she'd known for the last fifteen years, her eyes and nose burned at the thought of Bobby being shot and struggling under water, the way she'd found Henry...

"I'm sure Bobby will turn up." Henry's voice seemed tight and short. The tenderness they'd shared in the tunnels had vanished. The law enforcement ranger determined to prove himself had taken his place.

She shook her head and the damp braid whipped around and slapped her chin, keeping her together. She rushed forward and pulled out one of Bobby's specialty sandwiches—one she'd kept in her fridge for dinner—and a bottled water for herself and Henry. "Take this to go. I think we both need some sustenance to help us think straight after the day we've had."

And the night ahead, she reminded herself. She grabbed a knife, split the sandwich in two, and handed the drink and food over.

"I need you to call your aunt and tell her to stay put for now."

Nora nodded, averting her eyes. Why did the change in his demeanor hurt so much? She should've been used to it after the years since their breakup, but she'd felt so close to him after the events of the week. She bit her lip, not trusting that her untamed emotions wouldn't begin spilling over. If Maya was right, and they were all in danger, the only way the plan would work to take the drug ring down would be to go in hiding. Nora's chest tightened at the thought. What was the Lord doing?

When the walls seemed like they were caving in while they were stuck in the mines, she'd been challenged that it was time to go after the dreams she'd all but forgotten. And now? She might spend months, if

not longer, hiding and waiting without anything or anyone she loved. She cleared the emotion from her tight
throat. "What's going to happen to Maya after she officially gives her witness statement?"

He blinked. "If we get you somewhere safe, and we
do this right, she can get a lawyer and probably negotiate
a pretty good deal for herself." He leveled his gaze. "But
she's probably going to have to serve some time, Nora."

"I know." She'd hoped there would be another way,
but the truth steeled her nerves. She'd be spending a lot
of time praying for Maya's protection and heart through
it all. "I guess I needed to hear it, though. Do you know
where I'll be staying?"

His eyes flickered with gratefulness as he accepted
the sandwich and water from her. "Not yet. Possibly my
place at first. But only as a last resort," he added. "I'll
be back as soon as I can."

She flinched and watched his back retreat down the
hallway. He spun around. "Lock the door behind you,
Nora."

She nodded and closed the door. Staying with him
would be a last resort? She'd felt alone for most of her
life, but never *this* alone. The two people she had loved
most and lost had both been in front of her today as a
reminder of what she could never have. "At least You're
still with me," she whispered to God as a prayer. "I
could really use some of that peace right about now."

Henry ate with one hand during the straighter portions of the drive to the field office. At least he'd found

his spare, a set of keys magnetically hidden inside one of the U-channels in his roof rack.

The top priority was to get the appropriate gear and backup law enforcement set up to properly protect Maya and Nora. He debated calling the DEA—which might take some time to arrive—or an old friend in Coeur d'Alene, Deputy US Marshal Kurt Brock. The man had kept a federal judge and his granddaughter safe despite a private militia contract to take them out. He would probably help him find a safe house for Nora and Maya as a favor until the DEA stepped in. He just needed to find the man's number—since his personal cell phone had also been in his gear belt, now at the bottom of the river.

His arms twitched, wanting to take the turn that would take him to a fresh set of clothes and a hot shower. But Nora was right. The food and water must have been what he'd needed because he was regaining a new focus. He glanced at the clock. Sunset would be here before he knew it and, other than the dispatch radio in his truck, he had no way to contact anyone if he went home. The field office would at least have a phone and new gear, so he stayed on the county highway.

Never before had he been closer to solving Tommy's murder. Bringing in other law enforcement to make it happen stung, but it was time for him to let go once and for all and be a team player without his ego getting in the way. He exhaled a long breath. Ironic that the more confident he grew of his career and value, the easier it was to lay down his pride and let disapproval from others roll off his shoulders. If only he'd had that perspective when he'd first started his career. He'd probably be married to Nora by now.

The sudden regret was like a knife to his heart.

He hoped whoever was to be in charge of the drug ring investigation and Carl's involvement would at least give Henry's thoughts some consideration. Perry didn't seem like a real suspect, but he had been there at the time of Tommy's death and certainly had the type of power Maya would fear. Then there was the sheriff. He definitely had power, and he'd also been around when Tommy was killed. But he didn't seem like the type hungry for more money, more power.

His eyes widened. There was one person that fit all of the criteria and had the means and opportunity. How could he have missed it until now?

As he rounded the bend, a black SUV sat parked on the shoulder against a steep hill. The narrow highway was the only main road on the north side of the river, and it was illegal to park on the bank unless it was an emergen—

The SUV's hazard lights began flashing. He felt his forehead tighten as he pulled over. He really didn't have time to help someone out. He needed to follow up on the lead and, if he was right, Nora and Maya would be safe by nightfall.

Henry left the engine running, jumped out of his truck and rushed to the vehicle. He'd see if it was an easy fix, like a flat tire, and be on his way in under ten minutes. If not, he could at least alert Dispatch with the truck radio to send someone from the sheriff's department.

Lizzie Hartman stepped out of the SUV with a wave as he approached. "I'm so glad to see you. I wasn't sure what to do."

His steps slowed. For him, the hardest part of being in law enforcement was making the conscious effort to remain impartial. In trying to avoid giving special treatment to those he knew, he'd lacked compassion in the earlier years. These days, he made an effort to exercise an open mind and compassion with every citizen he needed to stop, and there weren't many people he disliked. Lizzie had been someone he counted as a friend. Until today. She'd abandoned Nora, having been poached by Frank's company.

"You're not happy to see me, though, are you?" Lizzie made an apologetic face. "It's not as if river guides make a lot of money, Henry. You don't know how many times I've turned down the offer to work at Frank's until yesterday."

He blew out a breath. "It's none of my business, Lizzie." Besides, neither rafting company would be able to start the spring season on time when the federal investigation started. He wasn't about to divulge that tidbit. "What seems to be the problem?"

"I have no idea. The engine was idling rough all day, acting weird, and then just stopped."

He gestured to the hood. "I can see if your battery just needs a jump or if someone can run out a sparkplug to you, but beyond that, I'm no mechanic."

She leaned back into her vehicle and he heard the pop before the hood lifted an inch.

"I'll hope for something easy," she said.

He ducked under the hood and reached to check the sparkplugs when the ominous click of a bullet going into a chamber set the hairs on the back of his neck on edge. He stared at the engine for a second, as if he hadn't heard. This wasn't one of the SUV models that kept the tire iron under the hood, but he searched for something to defend himself.

"Come on. Let's not make it harder than it needs to be. Hands up, McKnight."

He slowly straightened. "I really shouldn't have stopped for you."

She tilted her head, studying him. "It's too bad you got in the way. I always thought you and Nora made a cute couple."

His head suddenly exploded with pain that pounded into his temples and rushed down his spine. He dropped to his knees.

"You didn't have to hit him that hard," Lizzie said. "Tie his wrists and ankles, and get him in back before someone sees. I'll take his truck and park it in his driveway to buy us time."

Henry struggled to clear his mind and get his eyes to refocus, but the man had already tied and lifted him like a sack of potatoes. His shoulder hit the backseat before the man shoved the rest of his body in sideways. His head and ears still roared with throbbing pressure. But he could think straight enough to realize he'd been wrong. He'd never suspected Lizzie as the mastermind. Except, she didn't have the type of power Maya feared.

"Don't try to be a hero, Henry," Lizzie said as the SUV's engine came to life. He fought to sit up. A tall man with a baseball cap pulled down low sat in the driver's seat and Lizzie stood at the open back door closest to the hill. "If you want Nora to stay alive, you'll cooperate."

Henry gritted his teeth and blinked until his vision could focus on her face. Why would she assume he'd believe anything she said? "What have you done with her?"

"*I* haven't done anything, which is why you need to take me seriously. If you don't cooperate, she's automatically dead." Lizzie's voice shook ever so slightly.

"I'll cooperate," he finally said. He clamped his lips shut before he could speak the rest of his thought. *Until I see the moment when I won't.*

"Goodbye, Henry. Take him away, Lou." She slammed the door and the SUV took off on the highway, picking up speed, leaving Lizzie and his truck behind. He hadn't even had a chance to call in other law enforcement and still was without a weapon, yet he knew with every fiber of his bones that there was no way the drug ring would let him live after this. As soon as he saw his opening, he would take it. He'd die fighting to give Nora a chance at survival.

FIFTEEN

Nora zipped up her suitcase, assuming there wouldn't be any whitewater rafting where she'd be staying. It was time to stop procrastinating. She needed to call her aunt. She moved to grab her cell phone. Except the counter where she'd always put it was empty.

She rifled through the top drawer and, just underneath the photo of her and Henry, she found the small gun he'd bought her as an engagement gift. Her uncle—ex-uncle, she corrected herself again—owned the outdoor supply store and had instructed the manager to give Henry a deal on it. She wasn't legally allowed to carry it on the river, though, so she hadn't had it on her person since gun safety class. She'd never felt a need for it before now. She pulled the gun out, checked the safety and moved to peek outside her door.

No one was in the hallway—likely because Bobby had been right. The remaining employees had been poached. She fought against the way her body wanted to cave inward, ashamed at failing her aunt, and raised her head purposefully. She'd tried her best to save the rafting company. That was going to have to be good enough.

She ran out of the lodge and across the space to the back door of the office, looking over her shoulder as she went. Once inside the office, she breathed a sigh of relief. The cell phone was charged and ready. She set the gun down on the counter, within arm's reach, and dialed the number she'd been dreading.

With each ring, she saw herself as a fifteen-year-old showing up at the doorstep of a woman who didn't know the two children had existed. And after crying together, each with conflicted emotions, Linda had never threatened to send them into the social system. If Nora had been in her shoes, would she have done the same?

"Hello? Nora?" Her aunt's voice was accompanied by soft music in the background.

She could feel the emotion building at the base of her throat, the temptation to tell her aunt that everything would be fine warring with what she should say. She just needed to spit it out. "I'm afraid the business is not going to make a profit this year."

Once she began, Nora made sure she took the least amount of breaths possible. If Aunt Linda interrupted to ask questions, she might not get it all out. She started with Dexter's murder, and the connection to Tommy's murder, and ended with Maya's confession.

"So, all that to say you need to stay put for now for your safety, Aunt Linda, but once the case is wrapped up, you need to come back. I will no longer be managing the Sauvage Run." Nora blew out a breath.

The music in the background clicked off and her

aunt exhaled. "Wow. Well, I guess first I need to know if you'll no longer be manager because of the murd—"

"No. Dexter's death was only the catalyst to make me realize I've been waiting around for something that won't happen."

"Are we talking about Henry or Maya?"

Maybe both, Nora realized with a jolt. "I'm going to teach," she said, deftly sidestepping the question. "And, if the river ever gets safe enough to be open for visitors, offer my river guide services to the Bureau of Land Management during the summers."

"That's what you've always wanted to do, isn't it? Bobby tried to tell me, but I thought, if it was true, you'd have told me by now. Maybe I didn't want to see the truth because I had a lot to think over." She sighed. "And this all started with Dexter? I'm a little surprised. By your description, he really doesn't sound like the type of person we usually hire."

Nora reared back. "*You* wanted me to hire him."

"Me? No. I usually have Lizzie go through the applications first and give you her recommendations before interviewing."

Nora opened the frustrating filing cabinet. "No. You specifically wrote a note on the application." She flipped through the files trying to find the copy the police had made before taking the original. A file she'd never seen before flopped open, full of photographs. Nora hesitated, pulling one out. Her aunt and Frank, standing side by side, much in the same pose of Nora's photo with Henry. Except, she didn't see the same genuine happiness on their faces. Something else about the photograph bothered her, but she couldn't pinpoint it…

She dropped the photograph back into the file and flipped forward. "It was on a paper application, which is unusual for us. I didn't even know we had paper forms anymore."

"Oh! That one." Her aunt grew quiet for so long, Nora began to wonder if she'd lost the connection. "Well, I'm not proud of it," Linda finally said, "but I asked you to hire him out of spite."

"What?" Nora felt the twinge of a headache at the temples developing, perhaps due to her intense frowning.

"It was the last time I saw Frank, just after we'd signed divorce papers. He was trying to steal my employees again. We had words about it, but when I left, I took one of the applications on top of his pile when he wasn't looking. I… I'm sorry, Nora. It was a vengeful impulse. If he was going to take our employees, I was going to get one of his. I really wasn't thinking straight. It was actually the last straw for me. I knew I needed to get away. I couldn't even look at Lizzie, either."

"Lizzie? Why?"

"I…I didn't have any proof and didn't really trust my judgment at the time, but I suspected Lizzie of being one of the women Frank was having an affair with."

Nora's world spun on a dime and she couldn't focus on the rest of what her aunt was saying. Frank had moved from being a ranch hand and handyman to starting his own rafting business just after Tommy died. Linda and Frank hadn't started dating until a few years

later, after Frank's rafting company had been estab-
lished.

Frank had wined and dined her aunt right up until
they'd married. Everyone assumed his money had come
from good investments into the town and the surround-
ing ranches. His was the type of rags-to-riches story everyone loved. He'd worked two jobs at minimum ever
since high school, as he'd tell anyone who'd listen. His
rafting company instantly did better than Linda's, but
they'd always chocked it up to better salesmanship, even
though The Sauvage Run always had better customer
reviews. Soon, Frank had opened a small bait shop that
had eventually grown into a full-fledged outdoor gear
shop. A year later he'd opened a bistro. A year after
that, a coffee shop—

Nora gasped.

"What? What is it?"

"Frank owns a gun shop. I mean it's the outdoor
shop, but they sell guns."

"Yes. So?"

Frank could've forged paperwork to make it appear
Dexter had purchased a gun from his store. He would've
easily had access to guns. He was good at shooting. He
had access to rafting guides. He's a county commissioner. Did commissioners have a working relationship
with the sheriff's office?

"I have to let you go, Aunt Linda." She spun back to
the filing cabinet and found the photograph. "I need to
call Henry. I just remembered something. Just stay put
until you hear from us, okay?" She hung up before her
aunt could say goodbye.

Nora's hands were shaking. No wonder Maya was scared. Frank had the entire town's loyalty. The back door behind her creaked, but it had to be the wind. She had locked the door behind her the moment she'd entered. A quick glance over her shoulder to confirm—

"Put the phone down." The barrel of the gun was aimed right at her chest. Her uncle's face looked as calm and friendly as she'd ever seen. With his left hand, he slipped the back door keys into his pocket.

"You have a key." She didn't realize she'd spoken aloud until her uncle gestured with the gun. "Aunt Linda said she got your key back." The moment she spoke, Nora realized how foolish she sounded. Getting a copy made would've been too easy. That meant Frank could've entered the lodge office at any time to copy Dexter's handwriting from the paperwork. "You forged the suicide note."

His eyebrows pulled close. "Put the phone down, Nora." His voice, while still smooth, held a stronger edge to it.

She turned around and placed the phone on the counter, picking up the gun she'd set down with her other hand while her back was to him.

"I suppose I would've been disappointed if you didn't have your gun. I let him buy that gun at cost, you know. Set it back down and let's talk. I really don't want to have to hurt Henry."

Her spine went ramrod-straight. As she did so, she could see her reflection in the laptop's dark screen. That's how Frank had spotted the gun. She studied the counter in front of her. There was no way to get a message to anyone. The only things in front of her besides the laptop were the Closed sign on the counter, which faced the front door, and the How Can We Help? sign, which faced her.

Nora placed the gun on the keyboard, the barrel facing the word *Help* on the counter. It was a long shot anyone would understand her attempt at a message, but the tiny streak of rebellion washed any remaining exhaustion away.

She spun around, her back blocking the keyboard. "What about Henry?"

"Step closer to me and keep your hands up." The moment she did, Frank lowered his gun but still kept the barrel pointed at her legs. "Let's play a little game. You tell me where you're hiding Maya and the drugs, and I won't kill Henry."

She fought to keep her face steeled. He thought she had Maya? So, Maya had gotten away. But either that meant she was abandoning the plan to turn herself in and had disappeared off the face of the earth again, or she might be headed this way.

If Frank had Henry, then Maya would be walking into a trap. That left Nora with very few options. It was better to let Frank believe she was hiding Maya somewhere, though. Wasn't it?

"Tell you what… I'll tell you where the drugs are, and you let Henry go. Only then will we discuss Maya— and the only way I'm doing that is if Bobby is safe."

Frank quirked one eyebrow and smiled, which did nothing to ease her anxiety. The back door burst open and a tall, wiry man with a ball cap pulled down low over his eyes appeared. "No sign of her."

"All the rooms?" Frank asked.

"And under the beds. The ranger is in the backseat. Tied up and ready to go."

Go where? Nora tightened her lips together and sent up a silent plea for wisdom and help.

"Good. Because it sounds like we have a trip to make. Time for you to take me to the drugs."

Nora's quick glance out the window revealed the sun dipping precariously low to the horizon. "It's almost twilight."

"Then you better utilize the fastest routes." He glanced at the other man. "Get the raft ready."

"Maya said the leader of the drug ring was powerful." Nora's lip curled. "I never thought of county commissioner as a position of power."

"Now, see? Your aunt and Maya had vision, but not you. Never you." He shook the gun barrel at her as if it was his finger wagging, shaming her. "Disappointing. County commissioner was just the first step. Your aunt would've made a good governor's wife. But…depending on how you act tonight, maybe she still will. Couples often come back together after a crisis."

Nora recoiled as he smiled.

"I wonder if a bullet shattering a leg is the same as a rock. Do you think Henry would know? Maybe it doesn't hurt as much the second time," Frank mused, waving his gun around. "Either you get moving, or I might want to find out."

* * *

"You try to kick me and it'll be the last thing you do with your legs," the man grunted. He sliced a knife in between Henry's feet, released the rope and then took one lengthy stride backward, raising a gun at Henry's chest.

With his head still throbbing, and his wrists still tied together, Henry wasn't sure his balance would allow him to successfully kick the man's weapon away anyway. He would keep an eye out for any opportunity to overtake him.

"See? What'd I tell you?" Frank asked, almost cheerfully. The gun in Frank's hand pointed lazily at the middle of Nora's back. Henry's heart ran into overdrive, his neck burning. How could he so much as point a gun her way—

Beside him, Nora's face paled and her eyes widened. "His head. He's bleeding. What'd you do to him? You said you wouldn't touch him if I cooperated."

The wiry man gave a shrug to Frank. "Had to get him here first."

"That was before our deal, Nora."

The wiry man shoved Henry, clearly trying to force him to the raft waiting at the dock. The black SUV and another vehicle Henry didn't recognize blocked any would-be passerby from seeing the dock and their predicament.

Nora's pleading eyes met his. For all his time guessing at her thoughts, now the message seemed crystal clear. *Please cooperate.* He took a deep breath and almost asked if Frank had Maya as well, but something

told him he'd likely get a sarcastic or threatening re-
mark, so he remained silent.

"You want me to take you there this close to dark,
then I need your word," Nora said. "If I take you to the
drugs, you leave Henry and Maya alone."

"Fine," Frank said, too easily. "Time is ticking to
sundown, though. Lou and I were both river guides,
so we'll know if you try to flip the boat. We know all
the tricks. One wrong move and the deal is off. Are the
drugs still at the site?"

"Yes," Nora said weakly.

Frank ordered Nora to the back of the raft and sat
at her side. He instructed the man he'd referred to as
Lou and Henry to be placed at the front half of the raft.
Within moments, they hit the water. Nora shouted instructions with a fierceness Henry'd never heard from
her before. Even Lou had a paddle while Henry sat in
the front of the raft, helpless, with his hands tied. At
least his feet were free enough to hook his toes in for
additional support.

"Henry, grab on to the side handle."

He had to twist his torso as far as he could go, but
managed a two-fisted grip as a large wave slapped at
his chest. He sputtered but Nora kept shouting, taking
the hardest currents, the ones that would catapult them
down the river at top-notch speed. If not for the danger,
he would marvel at her abilities, the kind of praise he
should've been giving her all the while. His stupid pride
seemed to only be able to handle giving compliments
when he was on top of the world. Now, completely and
utterly helpless, he finally understood what Nora had

been trying to tell him. He set up walls for all the people closest to him, even his parents and brother. If he could finally set his ego aside, he could love with vulnerability. Not that he'd ever have a chance to test his theory. Too little, too late.

The river truly was wild, constantly changing. It didn't matter the training or equipment or planning, he had no control over the currents. So how was he supposed to help Nora get out of this alive? Especially while bound at the wrists. The river channel straightened, and the sun hovered at the horizon, sending blinding sunlight directly in their path.

He glanced over his shoulder. Nora seemed unfazed. Even in the calmer portions of the water, she pushed the gunmen to paddle harder, faster. They both had holstered their guns, and were squinting and sweating, but they never argued with or questioned her commands.

If Nora was trying to wear them out on purpose, she was doing a fine job. He'd have an easier time taking them down if they were tired. Except, exhaustion seemed to have seeped into his own bones after the day they'd had. Rapid after rapid, stroke after stroke. With each inch the sun dipped, Nora's voice grew weaker in authority.

Before he knew it, the sun had disappeared, leaving behind a mixture of oranges, pinks and blues. Nora's sharp inhale directed him to follow her gaze to the site where they'd tried to look for evidence about Tommy's murder just earlier that day.

"You murdered Tommy," Henry said, only half realizing he'd said the words aloud. He whipped his head around to look at the man in question.

Frank's good-natured-politician smile disappeared. The sunset's golden light reflected off the sheen on the top of his lip. "Mistakes were made in the early years."

"So, you admit it."

"That was before I realized I needed to manage my own rafting company, my own guides." Frank shrugged, confirming Henry's suspicions. The man would not talk so freely about murdering someone if he intended to let Nora and Henry walk away. "Using guides was a good idea with just a few problems. Tommy taught me I could only use guides that were local, from poor families they wanted to protect. In many ways, Tommy helped me become a success. Those in my business knew what his death meant."

Nora stopped paddling, her face slack. "Why? Why kill him?"

"He wanted out," Henry ventured. That would explain why Tommy had turned jumpy and nervous. He'd wanted out of drug running and was scared but not scared enough to admit what he'd been part of. Henry's gut churned with understanding.

"Except he tried to stiff me. Said he'd already sold my drugs to someone else and there was nothing I could do about it." Frank sighed. "Being a business owner can be tough. You have to know when to cut your losses."

"Is that how you viewed Dexter?" Nora asked, horror lining her features. "A cut to your losses?"

"Dexter should've never been on your rafting crew.

I don't know how that happened." Frank practically spat the words.

The last colors on the horizon disappeared, leaving behind a dark blue. The canyon walls added shadows, making any light harder to see within. Nora slipped her paddle into the water and shifted the raft toward land. They were almost to her hiding place. Once the men had the drugs, they'd be out of time.

"Carl's dead," Henry said, fighting to stall.

"Figured as much. And if you would like to join him, just keep opening your mouth." Frank's sneer took on a new edge, as if the darkness brought out the monster within.

"We had a deal." Nora jumped out of the raft and pulled it farther onto shore with Frank and the gunman already standing.

"No more sudden moves like that, Nora, sweetie." Frank's saccharine voice snapped the last shred of Henry's patience.

"Let's cut the false pretenses, Frank." Henry turned to Nora. "Don't give him what he wants. We all know he has no intention of letting us go."

"Sure I do. I always keep my promises." Frank winked, as if on the campaign trail. "You drop us off at the final take-out and you can go on your merry way."

"The take-out?" Nora crossed her arms over her chest. "We go our separate ways there?"

"You drop us off and continue on the river."

"That's Garnet Rapids, you know—"

"Yes, you get past that, and you're free to go. So, do

you want to take your chances on us shooting you both or with the rapids?"

Garnet Rapids would mean certain death, especially at night in high water. Even with someone as skilled as Nora, she wouldn't be able to manage the deluge.

"I thought we were using the tunnels," Lou said in a hushed tone.

"Until I talk to Maya, the tunnels are off-limits. She's a little too skilled at booby traps, thanks to your training." Frank flashed a clenched smile at Lou, his bleached teeth the most visible feature in the dimming light. He turned back to Nora. "Unless you're ready to renegotiate and let me know where you're hiding her?" Frank asked. "Everyone could be happy."

"We'll take our chances with the rapids," Nora said quickly. Henry paused for a second, confused at the interchange. Had Maya already showed up at the lodge and Nora had hidden her?

"Then enough chitchat. The drugs…?"

Nora walked ahead, leading them right to the tight space in between the cliffs and shrubs where Carl had been chasing them earlier. A dark figure stepped out of the boulders. "Freeze!" a male voice yelled.

A gunshot went off, but Henry couldn't see where it came from. Frank and Lou launched themselves at the other man. Henry ducked low. Now was the time to attack. He poised his back leg to launch him into the chaotic jumble of men to attack. Hands free or not, he would tell Nora to run.

She jumped in front of him, blocking his path. "No, don't. Please."

The newcomer to their group bellowed behind them. Henry knew that voice. Perry was involved? He struggled against his gut instinct to fight. He forced himself to still at Nora's quiet request. "Can I hope you have a better idea?" he whispered.

SIXTEEN

Nora had never been so glad she carried a pocketknife at all times. It was a necessary tool in guide work. The moonlight reflected off the blade as she slipped the knife handle between his hands. "Let's get you free, then wait for my signal."

"I think that man who yelled is Perry. He needs our help."

Sawing against the rope was proving harder than she thought. "You're no help to anyone tied up. Listen. Remember what Perry said about the snowmelt that first day? The—"

"Enough!" Frank yelled, spinning with his phone's flashlight beam shining into Nora's and Henry's faces before she could finish telling him her new idea. "I want the package, and I want it now, Nora."

She spun around, leaving the knife in between Henry's palms. "I want to see that Perry is okay." She had no idea why the man was there, but she finally believed he was innocent.

The beam of light hit Perry and his bloody shoulder. Lou held the extra gun that he no doubt had wrestled from Perry after shooting him. "He goes with us," she said.

"Fine. If you all make it through the Garnet Rapids, I wish you a happy life." Frank chuckled, with the knowledge that survival at that point would be impossible. She knew the only reason he wanted them to die in the rapids would be that their deaths would look like an accident of extreme thrill seekers rather than murder. The rapids would be at a Class VI or VII even by now. Impossible to navigate even in the best circumstances, especially in the dark. "The drugs, " Frank said as an order.

Nora's insides practically vibrated. They had one shot and it all relied on the fact she knew something her ex-uncle didn't. She got down on all fours, hoping Henry would have his hands free by now. If Frank went back on his word, she knew Henry would attack, gun or not. Whether he felt the same way or not, she couldn't deny she still loved the man. Her mouth went dry at the thought, but there was nothing she could do about it. She lifted up a silent prayer for survival as she reached into the darkness of the log and her fingers gripped the nylon bag full of drugs.

The moment she stood, Lou grabbed the bag and peeked inside with his own light. "It's all there."

"Good. Let's go." Frank waved the gun at them all, including Perry. She didn't need the light to confirm Perry wasn't well. She stepped to his side and acted as if she wanted to help him walk, while Henry trudged in front of them, his hands in front, pretending to still be tied up. At least, she hoped he was pretending. Her plan wouldn't work if his hands were still bound.

"Do you know if Bobby is okay?" she whispered out of the side of her mouth.

"No," Perry replied. "When I didn't hear from any of you, I went out looking. Had just found a mine entrance when—"

"He can walk by himself or die here," Frank muttered, grabbing Nora's elbow and giving her a push toward the raft.

Once they were all seated, she tried to steel her nerves. She didn't have time to share her plan with Perry or Henry. Ironically, this would be the only time when they would actually make it to the designated take-out all week, but she had no intention of delivering Frank there without a fight. And if Henry and Nora were both gone, no one would be left to warn Maya and Aunt Linda. She had to try.

The clouds shifted, blocking out even more of the moonlight. Bouncing over the waters, she was guiding blind yet could feel the current beneath the raft. She knew the river like the back of her hand but had never been tested in this way, especially with an upcoming new boulder and a set of hydraulics. *Lord, give me courage.*

"Only one more set of rapids to go through before the take-out, Nora. No funny business. I know the route, and I'll know if you deviate. Even in the dark."

"Fine, but I'm going to need your gunman to move to the opposite side of the boat to compensate. Perry and Henry can't paddle."

"I think we'll be fine," Frank countered with a warning sneer.

If ever there was a time to hold her ground, it was now. "When's the last time you've gone through these rapids with only two people paddling in the back? I venture you haven't. A kayak is very different than five people squished into a four-person raft."

Before Frank could argue any more, Lou shrugged and crawled on his knees across the raft to take the suggested place. "Move," he barked at Perry and Henry, and they slid across the thwart to her side of the boat.

She could feel Frank's eyes on her and fought to keep a nonchalant expression as she sliced the water with the paddle. Her shoulders and arms had never before burned with such intensity. If she ever sat in a rowing machine for a fun workout again, it'd be too soon.

She stared hard at the back of Henry's head as he tried to adjust his balance, sandwiched between the wounded Perry and the wiry Lou. It had to be hard to pretend his wrists were bound that close to the gunman.

"I know you can't help much, Perry, but you're going to have to keep your balance there," she called out. "You know the river, and you heard Frank. He expects us to go the *same* route we've *always* gone." She prayed Perry would get the meaning of her emphasized words.

He had been the one to warn her of the upcoming boulder that had changed the river, right before the bend to the final take-out. No one else had been able to scope the early spring waters yet. *Search for a new path or you're guaranteed to high side.* Those had been his words, right?

In the dim light, she was counting on just that. If they were ready for it, then they could adjust, and the two gunmen, even with their experience, would be catapulted into the water. But if Henry didn't understand her meaning, then it was very possible he'd be catapulted in the water, too. At least he had his hands free. Hopefully.

Perry gave her no indication of understanding unless she counted his moan when they hit a rolling wave. This was the final set of rapids for most trips and instead of a joy ride, it would be a roller coaster of terror. Henry looked over his shoulder and gave her a slight encouraging nod. Did that mean he understood?

Hope swelled in her heart as the current grabbed them and she felt the speed increase. Without moonlight, Frank would have no warning. As if hearing her plans, the wind gusted and the clouds shifted. A soft glow filled the canyon, but it wasn't enough to see more than dark shapes on either side. The dots in the rivers had to be boulders.

She realized, almost at the last second, the boulder was upon them. The raft jumped, then ramped almost straight up. "Now!" She shot upright, diving to the left and wrapping her hand around the strap on the side. Henry wrapped his arms around Perry, pinning them both to her side, as well. The wiry gunman yelled, hurling backward into the swirling water. The pressure of the raging waters held the raft almost on a diagonal, resting on the enormous boulder.

Her head snapped backward, and she felt her hair being pulled with intense force. She screamed as a strong grip slipped down her braid, yanking some hairs with it. The fingers moved to claw her arm.

"You're dead!" Frank yelled into her ear over the roar of the water.

* * *

Henry twisted toward Nora's scream, his left foot slipping and losing its stance on the bottom of the raft. Perry hugged the side with his good arm. Standing on such a steep angle proved precarious, but he had to stop Frank. He stepped over one thwart, straddling it, barely able to stay upright, twisting his body weight and slamming his fist into Frank's chin.

Frank's head snapped to the right, but he remained standing, though his balance wobbled as a forceful surge of water came over the lower edge of the raft and hit his ankles. He released his right hand from his hold on Nora and swung the oar at Henry's head.

Henry dipped his head, but the aluminum handle smacked his ear. The pain radiated down his neck. The momentum cost Frank his balance, and he used the bottom of the oar against the boulder to remain standing. Releasing his hold on the oar, Frank reached for the gun at his hip.

"The knife!" Nora shouted, barely hanging on to the side.

Henry's eyes widened and he struggled to grab the knife he'd put in his pocket. Frank raised the gun barrel to his chest as Henry's thumb flicked open the blade. He stabbed the sharp end on the inside of Frank's hand.

He howled and dropped the gun.

"Duck!"

Henry didn't question Nora's order. He dropped into a squat, hunched his torso over the thwart and looked up. Her oar spun in the air and slammed Frank in the chest. The man vaulted backward, airborne for half a second, until he dropped into the churning foam that obscured his foul obscenities as he disappeared down the swift waters.

Nora released a primal growl and planted the edge of the oar into the rock jutting above them, but the raft didn't budge. "We still need to get out. I'm not strong enough. Please, help!" Her shout sounded like half a sob.

Henry clashed with the pull of gravity to stand on shaking legs. He wrapped his hands next to hers around the oar. They pushed in unison against the unforgiving boulder.

Nothing happened for three full, torturous seconds as they wrestled against flipping into the same rapids the two men had disappeared into. Perry, still next to them, hung precariously on the edge of the raft, his eyes closed tight with pain and effort.

The raft shifted. Water sloshed against their heels and a wave bounced over the raft, drenching them, as the boat slid off the boulder and back onto the river. The water drained through the channels at the perimeter, leaving all three of them spent on the bottom of the raft, rolling with the remaining waves and panting with relief. "It worked." Her voice trembled. "It worked."

"Now what?" Perry yelled.

"I was hoping you could answer that." Nora sat up at the same time as Henry. Judging by her hunched form, every inch of her body felt as beat up as his did. She looked into Henry's eyes. "This is as far as I thought. I knew we couldn't make it through Garnet Rapids."

"That Lou guy might still have a working gun," Perry said.

"Frank's gun was lost to the river. I'm sure of that," Henry said. "At least we have only one potential gunman. Lizzie might be armed, though. And the guy waiting at the take-out spot," he added.

Nora blinked rapidly. She would have a lot to process over Lizzie's betrayal. "I think we can get off slightly earlier than the main sandy bank and maybe sneak past her."

"Let me worry about Lizzie," Henry said with a growl.

They rounded the bend, searching for the bobbing heads of Frank and the gunman. At least they had the upper hand in the boat. Flashing lights dotted the landscape just beyond the take-out point. Floodlights were aimed at the area right before the river dipped into Garnet Rapids.

"Rope!" a man in a law enforcement jacket yelled. A red bag soared out toward a bobbing head. Someone was trying to save Lou?

"Henry—" Nora gladly released the oar to his waiting hands. "The DEA is here. You called them?"

He reached for Nora's hand. "No. Someone else must have tipped them off. I've never been so thankful for help."

"There's one more," a search and rescue volunteer called out. Nora was so focused on the water, she didn't notice DEA officers rushing for their raft to help pull them up onto the beach until their hands gripped the sides.

"That man…they…those two men kidnapped us."

"They're drug runners," Henry said, finishing for

her. "One of them murdered a guide years ago. The Tommy Sorenson case."

Nora looked to Henry as the officers nodded, draped them in emergency blankets and led them to higher ground. "It's finally solved," she whispered, shaking her head. "And the murderer was with us the whole time."

Her eyes lifted and spotted her sister standing next to a squad car. "Maya?" Nora rushed forward, her muscles aching as she pushed through the sand. Maya reached her arms out wide, the only time her sister had made the first move to hug her since before their mother had passed. Her embrace felt so good. Nora laughed, tears dripping down her face. "I'm sorry, I'm getting you wet."

"Worth it," Maya said, her face dripping with tears. "I thought I might've been too late."

"I wasn't sure you were still going to come."

"I wasn't so sure myself. I was still debating as I drove to the lodge. I saw Lizzie driving away in Henry's truck. I knew right then I had to call the DEA direct."

Nora watched as Henry shook the hands of both officers flanking them and introduced himself. Their conversation became background noise, a comforting buzz as Nora tried to understand her sister. "You knew about Lizzie?" she asked her.

"I didn't know everyone on the payroll, but I learned about her recently." Maya hung her head. "Look, Nora. The DEA usually likes to take their time before showing up like this. I had to do a lot of convincing to get them to act so quickly, and it means, well..."

"You turned yourself in."

Maya grabbed Nora's hands. "I'll be serving some

time, but I'm going to point them to all the evidence I know of to put Frank and all his accomplices away for a long time. I set some traps that I need to help them disable." She offered a sheepish grin. "Hopefully that earns me at least a few points." She shook her head. "I'm sorry. I want to say more, but I think that's all I can handle right now."

The first sign of vulnerability she'd seen in her sister sparked newfound hope. Nora kissed her cheek. "We're sisters." She straightened. "I can wait. But how'd you know to show up here?"

"Bobby, actually. He spotted me when I looked for you at the lodge. He said he'd barely escaped someone trying to shoot at him and had to hitch a ride back. We both looked for you and when I found your gun pointing at—"

"The sign?" Nora exclaimed. "I didn't think anyone would get that."

"Like you said, we may have spent a lot of time apart, but we're still sisters."

An officer opened a back door to the DEA's SUV. "We should get going. We have a long drive and a lot of questions for you."

Maya nodded and gestured with her chin toward Henry. "Don't feel like you have to wait for me."

Nora followed her gaze and met Henry's smiling eyes. *Don't worry*, she thought. *I don't intend to.* But the real question swirling in her mind was if Henry was ready to open his heart again to her.

Maya slipped into the SUV and was driven away with the other officers escorting Frank and Lizzie and Lou.

"It's been quite a night," Zach gushed as he approached. "The DEA think Frank's arrest was done quietly enough, that with your sister's help, they can still do a raid on Copper City and catch all the guys coming to deliver and pick up the drugs this weekend."

Nora's head spun slightly with the influx of information as the sheriff approached with water bottles and protein bars for her and Henry. She sipped the water heartily, though her arm protested from the effort of even lifting the plastic bottle. The next few days were going to hurt.

The sheriff looked between her and Henry as Zach kept rattling off information, some of which she already knew about, namely Bobby being safe and waiting back at the lodge. "Zach, I think we can get their statements tomorrow," the sheriff finally said. "Why don't you head home before your wife thinks I let the wolves get you?"

Zach nodded solemnly and waved goodbye before heading for his vehicle.

The sheriff held out a set of keys to Henry. "Lizzie still had your keys, which corroborated Maya's story. Plus, the vehicles in the parking lot at the lodge. We dusted your truck for fingerprints. It's good to go now but still sitting in your driveway."

Henry's eyes widened. "I'm glad I had a team to back me up."

The sheriff offered a sad smile, likely still recovering from the news about Carl. "I'm going to see if the DEA is ready to wrap up here." He gestured at the three officers who appeared to be having a hearty discussion with Perry while he was being tended to on a stretcher. "I'll give you two a ride home when you're ready," he said as he walked away.

The coyotes howled and the wind blew. The moonlight streamed through the jostling leaves and branches. Henry stepped closer, his eyes never wavering from her face. Even though she knew he was thinking of what to say, his intense stare had the same effect she imagined it would on one of his suspects. She was ready to talk.

"So…do you think you're completely over that fear of water?"

He took another step closer and her feet seemed rooted to the spot. "Absolutely." The right side of his mouth lifted in the way that used to make her swoon. "As long as you're guiding."

"What?" She chuckled. "But you don't like to take orders from anyone."

"Oh, I've discovered going it alone is not nearly as fun as I made it look to be."

She laughed but stopped short as the paramedics released the hydraulic lift on the stretcher and began wheeling Perry in their direction. Perry saluted with his left hand, then turned his head to look behind him at the EMT steering. "I called it, you know. I knew they'd get back together."

The man gave an amused glance at Henry and Nora as her cheeks and neck flamed with heat despite the cool temperatures and her damp hair. The paramedics continued to wheel Perry to the waiting ambulance. "Uh, do you want to correct him or should I?" Nora asked.

Henry shook his head. "I'd really like him to be right."

The wind gusted against her back and she fought to stay upright. "What?"

He reached for her shoulders, offering her balance. "Nora, would you ever consider…" He looked up at the moon, as if searching for the right thing to say. "I mean… The point is…"

Her throat swelled with emotion. She didn't know what he was trying to communicate, but she was going to burst if she didn't get one thing she was sure about off her chest. "I love you."

His eyes widened and he looked in such a state of shock that if the paramedics were still there, they'd probably have been concerned. "You do?"

His gentle smile returned. He wrapped his arms around the emergency blanket still draped over her shoulders and pulled her closer. "I love you, too," he said softly. He bent and touched his lips to hers, warming her from her head to her toes. He pulled away, almost hesitant. "Are you sure? With everything going on you might need time to process."

"I've never been so sure."

He grinned. "Well, then that settles it."

She moved her arms to around his neck and kissed him with the promise of many more to come.

Three Months Later

"The Killer's just around the bend," Henry said. "How about we stop for a picnic?"

"It's not even noon yet, though. I thought you wanted to get farther down the river."

"I decided I can't wait."

She laughed. "I think Bobby has made you more sandwiches this season than I can count. You're not getting sick of them?"

He pointed to the bank as a way of answering. The river rafting season had started a month later than planned but, to everyone's surprise, Angela, from *World Travel Magazine*, had been happy to reschedule. The interview grew into the story about the rafting company's part in solving a cold case and shutting down a major drug operation.

In fact, Nora had been interviewed by more regional and national press reporters than she could count. But she hadn't minded. It was her parting gift to Aunt Linda and Bobby, who had teamed up to manage the rafting company together. They had plans to work all summer, then travel together to Chile to work the rest of the year. Maybe she would get the uncle she'd always wanted.

Nora slapped the oar playfully against the water, splashing Henry. He laughed and sent the water splashing right back at her.

When they reached the shore, he jumped out first and pulled the kayak farther onto the bank. Reaching for her hand, he helped her up. "I'm not really excited about the sandwich."

She stepped out and grabbed the picnic bag she had prepped and stored in her seat. "No?" She straightened to find him holding a bag of scones and a bouquet of flowers. Her mouth dropped open. "How'd you hide that in your kayak seat?"

"Very carefully." He beamed. "I wanted to properly congratulate the newest contracted third-grade teacher for Sauvage Elementary and also applaud your decision on a summer job working for the Bureau of Land Management."

After a whirlwind two months of substitute teaching, moving out of the lodge into a new apartment in town, and interviewing for teaching jobs, Nora'd applied to work as the river patrol during the summers. While it was a relief to no longer be in charge of a business, she longed to be on the river every day she could. She accepted the bouquet of wildflowers with an appreciative sniff. "I'm officially your coworker now," she teased. "Should you really be bringing me flowers?"

"First of all, you're not on the clock yet. You start tomorrow. Second, we're on forest service land so…"

She leaned her head back and laughed.

"What if we were married? Would it be okay to bring you flowers while we're coworkers then?"

Her breath halted and it took a second before her heart started beating again. Was this just a conversation about a hypothetical coworker romance? She didn't dare assume it was more.

"Nora, I want to do this right this time." He pulled out a little white box and opened it. Inside was a silicone ring, hot-pink, her favorite color. "I got this ring for you in case you might consider…" He frowned, as if nervous.

"Consider…?" she asked, her voice barely above a whisper.

He nodded. "Wearing it during the summer while you're on the river when you want to leave this at home." He dropped to one knee and opened a little black-velvet box. The sun caught the diamond and threw flashes of color onto the sand. "That is, if you'll have me. I love you, Nora. Will you marry me?"

She nodded, her throat tight with emotion. Henry straightened and wrapped his arms around her. "I love you, too, you know," she whispered. "So much." He pulled her close and kissed her, the top of the flower bouquet tickling their necks.

She set the flowers on top of the kayak and wrapped her arms around his neck. "Married or not, we probably shouldn't kiss while at work."

His eyes widened. "Then we better take full advantage of our days off."

She laughed and did just that.

* * * * *

*If you enjoyed this story, look for these other books
by Heather Woodhaven:*

Wilderness Sabotage
Chasing Secrets

Dear Reader,

Thank you for joining me on this wild ride with Nora and Henry. I loved learning more about the wild white-water experiences available in Idaho. While the Sauvage River may not exist, the inspiration for a lot of its best features comes from the Salmon River. I have a lot more respect for the work and training rafting guides and rangers do each summer to ensure their guests have a safe summer adventure.

Growing up with the verse in Galatians about bearing one another's burdens, sometimes I was so focused on being willing to help others that I forgot that no one could help with my burdens unless I was willing to share them, too. I don't have the same history as Nora or Henry, but I can understand their struggles. As I wrote their story, it served as a reminder that developing healthy relationships and boundaries takes a lifetime of practice. I can live each day with grace as I try my best, but know I'll likely make mistakes.

I hope you have a wonderful spring and are able to enjoy the beauty in the wild.

Sincerely,
Heather Woodhaven

Get 4 FREE REWARDS!

We'll send you 2 FREE Books plus 2 FREE Mystery Gifts.

Love Inspired Suspense books showcase how courage and optimism unite in stories of faith and love in the face of danger.

FREE Value Over $20

YES! Please send me 2 FREE Love Inspired Suspense novels and my 2 FREE mystery gifts (gifts are worth about $10 retail). After receiving them, if I don't wish to receive any more books, I can return the shipping statement marked "cancel." If I don't cancel, I will receive 6 brand-new novels every month and be billed just $5.24 each for the regular-print edition or $5.99 each for the larger-print edition in the U.S., or $5.74 each for the regular-print edition or $6.24 each for the larger-print edition in Canada. That's a savings of at least 13% off the cover price. It's quite a bargain! Shipping and handling is just 50¢ per book in the U.S. and $1.25 per book in Canada.* I understand that accepting the 2 free books and gifts places me under no obligation to buy anything. I can always return a shipment and cancel at any time. The free books and gifts are mine to keep no matter what I decide.

Choose one:
☐ **Love Inspired Suspense Regular-Print** (153/353 IDN GNWN)
☐ **Love Inspired Suspense Larger-Print** (107/307 IDN GNWN)

Name (please print)

Address _____ Apt. #

City _____ State/Province _____ Zip/Postal Code

Email: Please check this box ☐ if you would like to receive newsletters and promotional emails from Harlequin Enterprises ULC and its affiliates. You can unsubscribe anytime.

Mail to the **Harlequin Reader Service:**
IN U.S.A.: P.O. Box 1341, Buffalo, NY 14240-8531
IN CANADA: P.O. Box 603, Fort Erie, Ontario L2A 5X3

Want to try 2 free books from another series? Call 1-800-873-8635 or visit www.ReaderService.com.

*Terms and prices subject to change without notice. Prices do not include sales taxes, which will be charged (if applicable) based on your state or country of residence. Canadian residents will be charged applicable taxes. Offer not valid in Quebec. This offer is limited to one order per household. Books received may not be as shown. Not valid for current subscribers to Love Inspired Suspense books. All orders subject to approval. Credit or debit balances in a customer's account(s) may be offset by any other outstanding balance owed by or to the customer. Please allow 4 to 6 weeks for delivery. Offer available while quantities last.

Your Privacy—Your information is being collected by Harlequin Enterprises ULC, operating as Harlequin Reader Service. For a complete summary of the information we collect, how we use this information and to whom it is disclosed, please visit our privacy notice located at corporate.harlequin.com/privacy-notice. From time to time we may also exchange your personal information with reputable third parties. If you wish to opt out of this sharing of your personal information, please visit readerservice.com/consumerschoice or call 1-800-873-8635. **Notice to California Residents**—Under California law, you have specific rights to control and access your data. For more information on these rights and how to exercise them, visit corporate.harlequin.com/california-privacy.

LIS21R

A groan echoed in Ariel Potter's ears. Was someone
hurt? She needed to help them.

She heard another moan and decided she was the
source of the noise. The world seemed to spin. What was
happening?

Somewhere in her mind, she realized she was being
turned over onto a hard surface. Dull pain pounded the
back of her head.

"Miss? Miss?"

A hand on her shoulder brought Ariel out of the foggy
state engulfing her. Opening her eyelids proved to be a
struggle. Snow fell from the sky. Then a hand shielded
her face from the elements.

Her gaze passed across broad shoulders to a very
handsome face beneath a helmet. Dark hair peeked out
from the edge of the helmet and a pair of goggles hung
from his neck. Who was this man?

The pull of sleep was hard to resist. She closed her eyes.

"Stay with me," the man murmured.

His voice coaxed her to do as he instructed, and she forced her eyes open.

Where was she?

Awareness of aches and pains screamed throughout her body, bringing the world into sharp focus. She was flat on her back and her head throbbed.

Ariel started to raise a hand to touch her head, but something was holding her arm down. She tried to sit up, and when she discovered she couldn't, she lifted her head to see why. Straps had been placed across her shoulders, her torso, hips and knees to keep her in place on a rescue basket.

"Hey, now, I need you to concentrate on staying awake."

That deep, rich voice brought her focus back to the moment. Memory flooded her on a wave of terror. The horror of rolling down the side of the cliff, hitting her head, landing in a bramble bush and the fear of moving that would take her plummeting to the bottom of the mountain. She must have gone in and out of consciousness before being rescued. She gasped with realization. "Someone pushed me!"

Don't miss
Alaskan Rescue *by Terri Reed,*
available wherever Love Inspired Suspense
books and ebooks are sold.

LoveInspired.com

LISEXP0321